CW00501456

Healing Hearts

An Oak Harbor Series

Kimberly Thomas

ALL RIGHTS RESERVED. No part of this publication may be reproduced, distributed, or transmitted in any form or by any means, including photocopying, recording, or other electronic or mechanical methods, without the prior written permission of the publisher.

Copyright © 2022 by Kimberly Thomas

This is a work of fiction. Any resemblance of characters to actual persons, living or dead is purely coincidental. Kimberly Thomas holds exclusive rights to this work. Unauthorized duplication is prohibited.

Prologue

One Month Ago

"Thank you all for making the 'Social Media Transformation, Innovation and Common Man' conference the success it has become today. We couldn't have done it without your support and partnership."

Andrea looked out at the crowd of people applauding. A wave of pride washed over her at the realization she'd just hosted one of the largest social media conferences of the year. Even as the curtains were drawing, she had to admit she had not anticipated that it would've had such an exponential impact on drawing top-tier executives from major social media platforms, such as Facebook, Google, Twitter, and Reddit. She also wouldn't negate any of the accolades coming her way due to her role in all this.

She'd spent most of her adult life honing her craft of social media marketing, and this week had been a testament to how much her blood, sweat, and tears had paid off. The social media gurus and tech moguls in the room that attentively listened to her presentations and the staff that had been assembled to assist her in making the event a success had proven this.

As she walked backstage, many congratulations were directed her way from staff and guests alike.

"Andrea, you are beyond brilliant. I can't believe we didn't think of using you sooner," Tim, the managing director of SMW, the organization responsible for the conference, congratulated her. Grasping her hand, he shook it heartily. His light brown eyes stared back with a grin that bore straight, white teeth glistening like gems under the luminous lights.

This event had catapulted her into another realm, not that she was lacking in the department as in her own right she was described as the "Facebook Queen" for the inventive ways in which she advised on how to market with Facebook Ads and the success it had garnered among her clients and subscribers. She already had a cult following on her blogging and YouTube channels and had many connections in the field.

"Thanks, Tim. I couldn't have done it without you and the team," she spoke sincerely as her face lit up with her smile.

Tim gave her another dazzling grin.

"Before I forget, Kerry Davis wanted me to give you this." Tim fished out of his pocket a small, square card with the name Kerry Davis, Executive Social Media Marketing Director— WeChat, written in bold navy letters.

"Wow! This is great, Tim," Andrea expressed, flipping the card over to see that the number for the exec's direct line was printed on the back.

She'd been trying to set up a meeting with the messaging app's director for a couple of months now, but each time, she'd gotten the run around that she wasn't in the office or just wasn't taking calls at the moment. To be sought after by her now was another achievement she had to attribute to the level of exposure this conference had just given her.

"I have a few clients who have been pretty persistent about

getting tips on how to post their ads on this platform," she informed the man who stood before her, brows raised in interest.

"I wanted to talk with Kerry to get a better understanding of the app, but it's been an uphill battle," she explained further.

"Well, you've just proven beyond a reasonable doubt that you can roll with the best of them, so prepare for the accolades that are coming your way. Trust me, you're going to blow up even bigger than you are right now," Tim spoke sincerely.

Andrea's heart swelled as a feeling of warmth washed over her at the credence in which he spoke.

"Thanks, Tim," she accepted graciously, "I'm so grateful for your confidence in me."

"Oh, it's more than just confidence, Andrea. It's knowing what you're capable of and affirming the level of influence you have in this sphere."

Andrea could see the sincerity shining through his eyes, but there was something else there that she couldn't quite decipher.

Tim cleared his throat as he thrust his hands into his pockets.

"Listen, Andrea," he started slowly, facing her completely. "I was wondering if maybe after we're done here, we could maybe... that—"

Andrea tensed. She could already tell where he was going with the conversation. She didn't want to hurt his feelings, but she also wasn't looking for a relationship right now, casual or otherwise. The Carolina Herrera, green velvet, off-shoulder, close-fitting dress suddenly made her feel a little more exposed than it should have, especially sitting above her knees with four-inch Louboutin heels.

He tried to continue. "—you would like to join me for..."

"Andrea, there you are."

Andrea turned her head toward the voice to see Kathy

Bernstein, one of her associates, and another business owner walking in her direction. She was thankful for the distraction.

Looking back at Tim, she gave him an apologetic look just before Kathy interrupted them.

"I've been looking all over for you," Kathy said, looking between the two of them. She'd just realized that she'd intercepted a rather awkward conversation, at least on Andrea's part.

"I'll leave you two at it. I have a few people that I need to speak with before they leave," Tim spoke up.

"Oh, I'm sorry. Did I interrupt something important?" Kathy played coy, placing a delicate, manicured hand across her chest and looking from Tim to Andrea with concern.

Andrea fought to hold back the snicker at the woman's act.

"No, it's fine," Tim assured her with a tight-lipped smile. "It wasn't that important. We can discuss it another time," he offered, giving Andrea a hopeful look.

Andrea inclined her head to the side with an apologetic smile and a slight shrug of her shoulder as Tim gave her one last fleeting look before walking away.

"What did I tell you? I knew he was going to make a move on you. Now pay up," the woman who now stood directly in the position Tim had just been standing spoke in a matter-of-fact tone.

Andrea laughed at her colleague's antics.

"Kathy, you are incorrigible," she replied, shaking her head at the woman.

"But was I wrong?" Kathy asked with a raised eyebrow.

"No, you weren't."

Andrea sighed with relief at how close she'd come to hurting the feelings of the man that had given her the opportunity to host the biggest event of her entire career. She was grateful for his faith in her capabilities and for giving her a chance, but she didn't want to lead him into thinking she was interested in anything more than a platonic friendship.

"Anyway, I did come to break up your little hookup for a legit reason."

Andrea looked at her expectantly.

"Facebook's head has booked the El Chato restaurant on the fourth floor for an after-party and networking get-together, but only a hundred can get in. I just heard that your name is on the guests' list," her colleague informed her.

Andrea was surprised that there was an after-party as it hadn't been a part of the itinerary for the evening. She supposed a tech mogul like Facebook was entitled to do whatever they wanted. She was also pleased that she was added to the VIP list.

"If you don't want to be harassed by Tim or any of the other gentlemen I've seen eyeing you with stars in their eyes, then I suggest you stick with me. I'm a natural repellent of their affections. Who knows, maybe some of it'll rub off on you," Kathy continued to say.

Andrea could not deny that she was trying to avoid any form of entanglement, and if that meant sitting by the very chatty Kathy, then that's what she would be doing.

The restaurant, as unassuming as it looked on the outside, was more than enthralling on the inside. The first thing Andrea noticed as she stepped into the space were the floor-to-ceiling glass windows that provided the perfect view of the pink and blue skyline, the slightly darkened street below, and the glittering city spread out as far as the eyes could see.

Andrea and Kathy were ushered to their seat, where four other people, two of whom she recognized, were already seated. She realized that the natural arrangement was six people to a table.

After some time of making small talk with the people around her, Andrea excused herself to the bathroom.

She spent some time staring at her reflection in the mirror. A lot had happened in the past month. Her father had passed away, which had triggered her return to her hometown of Oak Harbor, the one place she'd pledged never to return to. Being back had brought up a lot of memories, both good and bad, but she couldn't deny how great it had felt to have had all her family around her. Her dad's death was still fresh, and she wasn't over it, but each day she was learning to cope with the loss.

Her mobile phone rang. Fishing it out of her small purse, she placed the device to her ear.

"Hello?"

"Hi, Mom."

A smile danced across her lips at the sound of her daughter's voice. "Hi, sweetie. How are you?" she asked, already perking up.

"I'm really good. How was the conference?"

"It was amazing." A huge smile graced her lips while she recounted to Aurora the success of the conference and her own elevation by it.

"I'm happy for you, Mom. I know how hard you've worked for this. You deserve it," her daughter expressed.

Andrea's daughter's support warmed her heart. Since the day she found out she was pregnant with her, it had always been just the two of them. That was, until Rory, the nickname Andrea had used since she'd been two, met her boyfriend James, and the two moved to a different state for work. Nevertheless, the bond they had was still very strong. Not one day went by that they didn't call or text to make sure the other was okay.

Even though she now had to share her daughter's affections with someone else, she had no complaints. James was a lovely young man that loved her daughter and treated her as if she was the most important person in his life. At twenty-three and twenty-five, they were young, but their level of maturity was reflected in the way they took care of each other. She never got the chance to experience anything like it, but her daughter was fortunate to find it so early in her life, and for that, she was grateful. If anything happened to her, she knew there was one person aside from her that would always be there for her daughter.

Andrea remembered when Rory was just six years old and had confided in her how she was going to marry a handsome prince and have a big family so they would never be alone again. It seemed her daughter's dream was shaping up just as she'd imagined it. She'd loved James, and she knew that someday in the future, he would indeed officially turn her daughter into his princess.

Her mind flashed to an unpleasant memory just then, causing her to grip the phone a little tighter at its sudden, unheralded presence in her mind. Shaking it away, she focused on the conversation once more.

"So, what's going on with you?" she asked.

Andrea worried at the silence on the other end of the line. *Why was her daughter now so hesitant to speak?* "Rory?" she prompted.

She heard her daughter draw in a deep breath before slowly releasing it.

"Mom, I know you only want what's best for me, and I know that you've always respected my decisions. It's just... even though I know the type of person you are, I'm not sure how you'll take this news," her daughter spoke frantically.

Andrea's heartbeat started to race as she considered her daughter's words.

"What is it, sweetie? You know you can tell me anything. I promise I won't judge," she said reassuringly.

"I know, Mom. That's why I love you so much," Rory

humbly gave out. "James asked me to marry him, and I said yes."

"Oh, honey. That's great news. You know I love James."

Andrea heard Rory sigh through the phone. Her words had relieved her daughter. "So, you're happy? We have your blessing?"

"Of course, Aurora. Always. I love you. This is such wonderful news."

The two chatted for another twenty minutes as Rory rambled on about her engagement and other details. She was excited for her daughter and happy that she'd found love.

There would be at least one thing to celebrate, Andrea thought to herself.

Chapter One

Present Day

Andrea yawned, and she stretched her tired limbs in the middle of her mahogany canopy framed California king-sized bed. It had been an impulsive buy. At the time, she'd gone couch shopping for her apartment and had fallen in love with how huge and comfortable the bed looked. She'd imagined how great it would look in her master bedroom compared to the full bed that didn't quite fill the space adequately. The instant she sank into the soft cushiony mattress that enveloped her frame and made her feel as if she were lying on clouds, she knew she had to get it.

As she nestled further into the softness now, feeling the urge to go back to sleep, she wondered if it had been a wise buy after all. She needed to get up. She had to go into her office to send off some important emails and finish her blog, but between the mattress and her comforter forming the perfect cocoon, all she wanted to do was fall right back to sleep.

Suddenly her alarm went off, reminding her of the reason she'd awoken in the first place.

"Ugh!" She breathed in frustration, still not making a move to get up. The incessant noise continued without interruption. When she couldn't take it anymore, she rolled over in the bed to look over at the small vintage machine on the bedside table that was making it hard for her to just curl up and fall back into a blissful sleep.

Reaching over, she tapped the knob to stop the ringing and brought her hand back to her side. She inhaled deeply before slowly releasing the air through her lips. Scooting to the edge of the bed, she swung her legs over and stood to her feet.

It was time to start her day.

After taking a quick shower, she dressed in a white, three-quarter sleeve blouse tucked into black high waist slacks. She stood before the shoe section of her closet for quite some time, contemplating which one went well with her outfit. She finally settled on the black wedge-heeled opened-toe shoes with cutouts at the sides and back.

Walking out of her closet, she slid the door back in place and took advantage of the floor-to-ceiling mirrors that took up the entire wall of her walk-in closet. Feeling satisfied with her look, she snatched her laptop off the small work desk at the other corner of her bed and stuffed it into the laptop bag on the chair before raising it to her shoulder along with her black Hermès handbag she'd received as a gift from one of her clients.

Stepping out of her bedroom, Andrea moved past the living room and stepped into the kitchen on the other side of the open floor plan design. Grabbing a tangerine from the fruit basket on the counter, she made her way to the front door. She would stop by the Starbucks on 172nd St., less than ten minutes away from her apartment in Cedar Pointe, and get a coffee and maybe a pastry.

Instead of taking the elevator, Andrea walked down the five

flights of stairs to get in some early morning exercise. When she finally made it to the ground floor, she made her way across the lobby and stepped through the sliding glass doors. She sauntered to the covered carport adjacent to the building and headed for her designated parking spot. Andre settled into her olive-green Jeep Wrangler before driving out toward the exit of the complex.

"Good morning, Ms. Hamilton. How are you today?"

"Good morning, Harold. I'm fine, thank you." Andrea smiled politely at the friendly security guard, who was smiling broadly at her as he released the automated gates for her to drive through. "How's your wife doing?" she paused midway through the exit to ask.

"Oh, she's fine. Just her poor old left knee is giving her some pain because of arthritis, you know," he answered.

"I'm sorry to hear, Harold."

"Don't fret about it now. She'll be fine soon. It comes and goes," he assured her.

"All right, Harold. Keep me posted," she requested. "I'll see you later."

"Bye, Ms. Hamilton."

Andrea pulled out of the complex and made her way along Cedar Avenue before turning onto 172nd St. A few minutes later, she pulled off the main road and made her way over to Starbucks. When she entered the establishment, only two other people were before her, and only a few tables were occupied. She rejoiced internally. Usually, whenever she made it to Starbucks at this time, the place would be teeming with people trying to get their daily coffee fix before their busy day started.

"Hi, welcome to Starbucks. What can I get you?"

Andrea smiled at the young woman whose name tag read "Joy," enjoying her aura.

"Hi, um, can I have an espresso macchiato and..." She

3

paused, looking over at the pastry display. "Can I have a bagel and cream cheese to go, please?" she finished.

"Sure thing. That'll be six ninety-five."

After paying for the food, Andrea moved to a spot where her name would be called once her order was ready.

After collecting her items, Andrea walked back to her Jeep and pulled out of the parking lot onto the road. Ten minutes later, she was at the three-story building that was rented as office space. Her office was located on the second floor at the east end, an ideal position as she was able to take advantage of the natural light that came through the glass panels that formed the entire east wall and the adjacent wall facing outward.

Her office was vibrant and modern, symbolic of her personality. The furniture and upholstery of the room were an analogous mixture of colors that complemented each other very well: from the multicolored area rug, the aqua-colored armchair, the olive-green work desk and chair, to the mustard-colored walls interrupted by evenly spaced light-gray vertical lines that completed the box-shaped office. The only mute colors in the space were her blogging and recording equipment which ranged between white and gray, the large black and white office desk holding two large monitors, an Ipad, and a Rode NT-USB Condenser microphone. To anyone else, the room would probably look a little chaotic, but for her, it worked.

The office was her home away from home. It was where she did her greatest work, and her creativity was unhindered. She chose to have an office away from her house almost five years ago because she'd recognized that her level of productivity was not where she wanted it to be. A friend and associate had suggested she rent an office space. It turned out to be the best decision she'd made.

Andrea set her laptop and planner in between the two monitors and went to switch on the softbox lights and the diffuser. Today she wanted to vlog about steps to take to attract the right kind of people in one's life that would foster healthy relationships. It was something new and a follow-up from her last video, giving her subscribers tips on how to start seeing themselves in a positive light and shedding the negativity perpetuated by themselves and those they had been associating with. She'd received a lot of positive feedback, with some people sharing the success they had using her suggestions. This was the part of her job that she loved— being able to help people know that there was still hope even after life-altering circumstances.

First thing first, however, she needed to respond to some emails from her clients and check up on the ads she was running for them. With her planner at hand, she was prepared to make notes on which ads were still running successfully and which ones might need tweaking to their content and visibility. This was her main job, the one that paid her bills and gave her a nice cushy bank account.

The first email she opened was from Ziccardi, a well-known jewelry store that had commissioned her to run ads. They were requesting their invoice.

She decided to get on it right away. Just as she brought up her business invoice template, her cell phone rang. Raising herself from before the screens, she made her way over to her desk, where her cell phone sat.

Andrea noticed the caller id read "unknown" but thought nothing of it as she was used to getting those calls from potential clients.

"Hello?"

She felt the blood drain from her face from the initial shock of who was on the other end of the call. Soon anger replaced her shock, and she gripped the phone tightly, causing her knuckles to go white as her face likely reflected her annoyance.

"Why are you calling this number?" she seethed. "Save it. I don't want to hear it," she blared, interrupting whatever the person was saying. "You had your chance over twenty years ago to pick up the phone and call me, and you didn't. So maybe you should've kept that same energy until the day you go to your grave. Don't ever call me again. Stay away from us." With that, she ended the call, raging. Steam rolled off her in waves as she paced back and forth, shaking, her breakfast and plans forgotten at that moment.

So much for the peace she'd felt earlier. Suddenly her phone blared again.

"I thought I just told you to never call my phone again," she barked into the receiver.

"Well, hello to you, too, Sis."

Instant regret filled her at the sound of Cora's surprised voice.

"I'm sorry, Cora, I thought you were someone else," she apologized.

"I'd hate to be that other person who's got you in such a tizzy," her sister half-joked.

"I'm really sorry, Cora. I should have had a better handle on my anger. It's just that the call earlier caught me by surprise, and let's just say it was a blast from the past that I don't want to revisit," she explained.

"Yeah, I know what you mean," her sister said with understanding.

"If Joel called me now, considering all that he's done up to this point, I'd probably go off on him just the same," she revealed.

Andrea sighed, resting her hip against the desk.

"I'm really sorry about Joel, Cora. What he did to you guys was so wrong, but on the bright side, at least it has opened you up to the possibility of finding love again with a certain contractor," she encouraged.

"Jamie's a great man... a good friend."

Andrea picked up on the hesitation in her sister's voice.

"Cora, no buts," she halted her. "You deserve this. I know you're trying to be cautious, but please don't try to make excuses to ruin what is happening between you two."

When her sister didn't immediately respond, she pressed on. "You deserve to be happy."

"Thanks, Drea," Cora spoke up gratefully. "I'm actually calling to see if you're still coming home tomorrow," Cora continued carefully.

Andrea's heart slammed against her chest. She'd been putting off going back to her childhood home to help Cora take care of the inn and her mother for the past couple of weeks. It had been one thing to attend her father's funeral in the town she'd grown up in and had never returned to after she'd left so long ago. Now, she knew that to be back there for any amount of time would bring up unwanted memories and emotions she'd chosen to bury a long time ago.

"Mom needs you, Drea," Cora stated after some time of silence. "I need you," she murmured in a resigned voice.

Andrea could hear the vulnerability in her sister's voice, and it filled her with guilt that she'd left all the responsibilities to her alone.

"I am," she promised. "I'll be there tomorrow by four in the afternoon."

"That's wonderful news," Cora replied with relief. "Oh, there'll be a barbecue with Uncle Luke, Aunt Maria, Aunt Stacy, some of our cousins, and their kids will be here too."

"All right, I'll try to make it in time," she agreed. "I guess I'll see you tomorrow."

"Okay, Drea. I'll see you tomorrow."

Chapter Two

"Remember, not everyone is traveling on the same wavelength as you are. It's okay to treat your paths crossing as a chance meeting, but there's no need to make it more than it is. Let them go; you're saving yourself a lifetime of pain and regrets. Finally, always take care of you, and fight the urge to make the same choice that didn't work the last three times you tried. You are special, and you're unique. Own it."

After the final word left her mouth and the camera was switched off, Andrea released a long, heavy sigh and slouched in her chair.

Her mind flashed to the conversation she'd had with her sister less than an hour ago. She'd been putting off going back to Oak Harbor, not ready to dredge back up the memories and the regrets they perpetuated. But she heard the despair in Cora's voice. If she was honest with herself, she knew the moment had been coming. She needed to go home for her mom and to help with the inn.

Her phone rang just as she slipped her bag onto her shoulder. Balancing the device between her ear and her shoulder, she answered, "Hello?"

"Hi, darling."

"Hi, Kathy," she greeted her friend while exiting the building.

"I heard Tim didn't take it well when you turned down his offer to be second vice president at SMW."

Andrea released a small chuckle. "Took you long enough to call. I knew you would get a kick out of the drama."

"You know me too well, darling— I live for the drama," Kathy replied in a southern drawl.

Andrea shook her head in amusement.

"So, what happened? I only heard that he was in a sour mood for the rest of the day after you left his office," her friend prodded.

Andrea released a long, tired sigh as the day in question came before her. "I've never seen him that angry," she revealed with a swift shake of her head. She was still in disbelief that this was the same man that had been so instrumental in catapulting her fame in the social media stratosphere tenfold. "He literally called me an opportunist who screwed over the hand that stretched out to feed me for the next best thing."

"He didn't," Kathy exclaimed, her voice rattling with shock.

"He did." Andrea laughed. "He then went on to say that I would live to regret my decision, and when that happens, don't think that he'll be there to bail me out. Being a part of his company is a one-time offer that won't ever happen again."

"But he's forgetting you were doing fine on your own," Kathy reasoned. "You don't need him, Andrea. He's just salty because you turned down his offer to go out with him. That's why he's taking it so personally."

Andrea sighed. "Well, it doesn't matter now. I'm going home, and I think I might be there for a while."

"Home as in back to Oak Harbor?" her friend questioned.

"Yes. My mom is not doing so well, and my sister didn't say it, but she really needs my help. That means I'll have to pass on a few of my clients to lessen my workload," she explained.

"I'm sorry to hear that, honey. I hope it all works out. You can send a few of them my way if you like. I have a bit more time."

"Thanks, Kathy. I appreciate it."

"No worries. You go and visit your family. Give me a shout when you get back or if you come back."

After hanging up, Andrea placed her belongings in the back of her Jeep, pulled out of the parking lot, and headed for her house.

Stepping through her front door, Andrea placed her bags on the console table in the hallway of her apartment and made her way to the kitchen. She poured herself a glass of the chilled red wine from the refrigerator and rested her back against the kitchen island to enjoy the slightly tangy, fruity taste as she swished it around the caverns of her mouth.

Pouring the remaining wine from the bottle into her glass, she headed for her bedroom and went straight over to her closet. She slid the door open before stepping inside and began packing.

After packing for the past half hour, she changed into her cycling gear and grabbed her bike from the guest bedroom before heading downstairs to her Jeep. Andrea had always needed to burn calories, whether it be with a run or cycling. She needed this ride; she felt overcome with emotions. She just needed to do something to clear her mind.

* * *

Andrea could feel the muscles in her legs tense as they guided the up and down motion of the pedals of her bike. The wheels yielded to the pull of the chain, demanding their movement and propelling the machine forward. She loved the freeness she felt as her lungs expanded and contracted from the fresh air that glided against her skin when she picked up momentum. She loved the resistance her muscles felt as her legs worked hard to keep the bike in motion and her body atop it— to her, the experience was far more exhilarating than strength training in a gym.

Where the trees thinned, she was blessed with the view of the planes making their ascent into the evening sky and those making their descent toward the runway at Ronald Regan Airport.

She stopped to rest a bit. She straightened up to look across the horizon as her thoughts switched to her daughter. An instant smile graced her lips as she thought about how proud she was of Rory. Despite not growing up with a father, Andrea wanted to believe that she'd raised her daughter well.

Her thoughts went to Rory's father, and instantly, her mood changed as she remembered his call earlier. *What had she seen in him all those years ago?*

"Come on, Drea. It's good money. These big parties always are. Plus, there'll be a lot of movie stars there. You'll get to boast that you've met people like Sallie Field and Rob Lowe."

Andrea looked back at her friend with wary eyes. "I don't know, Kimmy. Huge parties aren't usually my thing," she spoke hesitantly.

"But it's good money," Kimmy reiterated.

"Yeah, it is, but usually, these parties get out of hand. You know most of the movie stars are into hard drugs and liquor, and I'm not looking to be around that, not again," She shivered with the memory of her ex-boyfriend whom she'd followed out here. He'd been into all the drug-infused parties and had taken her to one once. She hadn't liked it. It was a memory she wished she could erase.

"I hear what you're saying, but I don't think anything like

11

that is gonna happen. Angie said this party is like a celebratory gig for some up-and-coming movie director. His latest film was a box office success, so the film crew and actors are just celebrating with him," Kimmy reasoned.

Andrea still wasn't convinced.

Her friend sighed. "Look, if we go and you're not comfortable, we'll leave. I promise."

She looked at the seriousness on her friend's face and felt a prickle of guilt. Kimmy had been the one who'd gotten her the waitressing job back at the pub and had allowed her to stay with her after her breakup. The least she could do was repay her kindness by taking the gig with her.

"Okay. I'll do it," she conceded.

"Yay!" her friend exclaimed excitedly as she threw her arms around her.

"Thanks, Drea. You won't regret it, I promise."

That's how they had ended up at the mansion and how she'd ended up meeting David.

She'd been walking with a tray of champagne flutes across the pool deck when she lost her footing and found herself teetering toward the welcoming water of the pool. A strong arm wrapped around her waist, pulling her back as a hand held the tray. Her back was pressed against a firm chest, and the tray was being balanced by a hand corded with muscles.

"Are you all right?"

The smooth baritone of the man's voice caused her to shiver involuntarily. Andrea found herself nodding instead of responding with words. Her throat felt parched, and the smell of his cologne mixed with his natural male scent tickled her nose and seemed to befuddle her thoughts.

The arm loosened from around her but only to pivot her until she was facing a tall gentleman with the most unusual hair color— ginger— but that somehow was just right, especially *complemented by the greenness of his eyes set in a perfectly sculpted face. She swallowed involuntarily.*

She saw his lips move, but she couldn't comprehend what he was saying. She shook her head to clear the fuddle when the man waved a concerned hand before her face.

"I'm sorry, what were you saying?" she asked, her voice coming out short and breathy.

The man smirked, a dimple appearing in his chiseled jawline.

"I was asking if there is someone I need to duel in order to be your permanent knight in shining armor?"

She swooned, her cheeks becoming uncharacteristically red.

Andrea shook her head to clear the memory and further disappointment at how gullible she'd been.

An hour and a half later, she was back where she'd begun her journey. After mounting her bike on her Jeep, she headed for home.

After taking a shower, she decided to pack up her camera and equipment to take with her to Oak Harbor. Going back into the closet, she used the short stepladder to reach one of the top shelves, where she kept the kit with her digital camera and zoom lens. She could see it pushed further to the back of the shelf. On her second try to get it, she hooked her finger around the strap of the bag and pulled. The bag came over the edge of the shelf along with a small safety chest that crashed to the floor, spilling its contents. Stepping down, she leaned over to inspect the items.

Moving aside some old trinkets and souvenirs from her childhood, Andrea reached for the small, partially obscured picture. It was one of her father, a wide grin plastered on his face as he stood in front of his old boat that was docked in their backyard, out on the harbor. Standing on his left was a young Andrea with an equally radiant grin as her blue eyes glinted. She'd only been ten then.

She ran her thumb over her father's face as a tear slipped from her eye and ran down her cheek.

She remembered they'd gone fishing in the harbor. Her sisters had gone to Uncle Luke, Aunty Maria, and their cousins without her because she had a slight fever. Becky had suggested she stay home. However, within the hour after the others had left, her temperature had returned to normal. Her father decided to take her out on the water to take her mind off the disappointment of not going with her sisters.

It had been one of the best days of her life. They had caught a few yellow perch and one Chinook salmon. Her overall count had only been two small yellow perch, but she held them up proudly while posing beside her father, who had a good catch. The two smiled broadly at her mother, who stood behind the lens, taking the photos.

The memory was such a pure one back then, but as she continued to look at the picture, she recalled that it was also the day she'd learned about her father's plans for their future, that it didn't go beyond the scope of them running the family business— the same business that had driven all three girls from home and severed their relationship with their father.

Another sob escaped her lips as she raised her hand to her mouth to stem the sound. She wished she'd been there to at least say goodbye to him, to let him know that she still loved him. All she had now were photos of happy times lost and a lifetime of regrets.

"I'm coming home, Dad. I know you're not there anymore, but I'm coming home." As she spoke, she stroked the photo and placed a loving kiss on the glossy image. "We'll take care of Mom. I promise."

Chapter Three

Andrea had been driving for over thirty minutes when she spotted the sign that indicated the highway was just a few miles away from where she was. She watched the road keenly, not wanting to miss the turn-off that would take her onto the interstate. Two minutes later, she was on the highway heading toward her childhood home.

Her phone rang. Looking over at the device mounted on the air vent, she realized that it was her daughter calling. Andrea tapped the answer button and then greeted Rory.

"Hi, sweetie."

"Hi, Mom." Rory's chirpy voice filled the interior of the Jeep as she greeted her mother.

"You sound extra bubbly this afternoon," Andrea observed. "What's up?"

"I am," Rory agreed. "Remember I was telling you that James and I wanted to have our wedding reception at the Le Meridien, but they were completely booked for all of next spring?"

"Uh-huh," Andrea mumbled, waiting for her daughter to finish her statement.

"Well, we got the call today that they can pencil us in for March third after another couple dropped the appointment," Rory replied, unable to contain her excitement.

"Wow, sweetie, that's great news," Andrea responded, happy for her daughter.

Even though the wedding was a little more than eight months away, Andrea knew how important it was to get some of the most pertinent items, such as the wedding venue and guest list, out of the way. You could end up rushing and feeling frustrated the longer you waited to sort those things out. She knew because event planning was something she occasionally did. She also knew how much her daughter had wanted the glitzy upscale restaurant that was widely sought-after and usually heavily booked during the spring for wedding receptions, bridal, and baby showers.

"Yeah, I know. James doesn't understand why I'm so happy about this, so I couldn't really get him to feel the joy I felt. I thought it was best I called you. You would understand."

Andrea laughed at her daughter's reasoning.

"So, how is my favorite son-in-law?"

"James is great, Mom. Barring his lack of understanding of the importance of getting the best reception venue, he's been so wonderful and supportive," Rory spoke dreamily.

Andrea smiled in satisfaction. She was happy Rory had someone to lean on at this time, someone who seemed to always put her needs first. Andrea could not have asked for a better partner for her daughter.

"He has this huge case he's working on, and it's been really stressing him out. I think he may of bit off more than he can chew. It's a really big opportunity for him to move from junior attorney to an associate, though, so hopefully, he'll push through," she informed her mother.

"That's wonderful, honey. I'm sure he'll manage. He always does."

"I'm just happy he still finds time for me, to make me feel special. I'm trying to take care of as much of the wedding arrangements as I can by myself so that he doesn't have to worry about this too. I need to send out our save the dates soon. Speaking of, do you think I should send any to my cousins? I already made all of them along with Aunt Cora, Aunt Josephine, and one for Grandma, but I wasn't sure if—"

Andrea sighed inwardly at the uncertainty in her daughter's voice. She could see how much she wanted to get to know her family, but with so many years of barely keeping in touch, she could understand how unsure Rory felt about it, probably not wanting to appear out of character, inviting them like that. They had spent the few days they had been in Oak Harbor getting to know each other, but it was hardly enough time to build a bond with anyone.

"You should," she encouraged her. "I'm sure they would appreciate the gesture."

"Okay, great."

She could hear the sigh of relief in her daughter's voice as if she'd been holding her breath, waiting for Andrea's weigh-in.

"So, where are you? I hear cars passing by."

"Oh, I'm actually on my way to Oak Harbor. I promised Cora that I would go back and help her with the inn and with Mom," she explained. "I should have let you know when I was leaving. Everything has just happened so fast."

"Mom, it's fine. I understand," Rory assured her. "How long will you be gone for?"

"I'm not sure, sweetie. I packed for at least a month, but I think I'm going to be there for a while," Andrea replied. She hadn't given much thought to that, and she still wasn't sure.

"If I need you, I know where to find you then. I'm happy you're getting this time to reconnect with them."

Andrea wanted to hug her daughter right now for how mature she'd become but instead settled for, "I love you, Rory."

"I love you, too, Mom."

"Next time, I want to hear my son-in-law on the line," she playfully warned her daughter.

Rory laughed at her mother's antics. "Okay, Mom, next time."

After she ended the call, her mind flashed back to the reading of the will. The day she found out that despite her father's threats and coldness toward her and her sisters, he'd still left the business to them. The biggest shock, however, had been the revelation that their mother was struggling with a life-threatening disease. ALS was no joke. The research she'd done had left her with nothing but helplessness and dread. Perhaps this final act, though, was their father's way of bringing them all together as a family so that they could heal and rebuild their family bond.

She remembered the letter he'd left for them and how the letter had proved his love for them. She remembered curling up in her old bed and re-reading it to herself.

Dear girls,

If you are reading this letter, then I suppose it means I'm dead. What can I say that will make this moment any better for you all?

Firstly, I want you to know that I love you very much. I've never stopped. I know, in the end, it seemed like the opposite and I am sorry for that. I was proud, selfish, and stuck in my old ways.

My wish is that you will take care of your mother, be there for her, and make her comfortable. She's the only woman I've ever loved and this is my final act of love for her. If you choose to sell the property after she's gone, I understand.

Be good to each other, love each other and most importantly, stick together.
I love you.
Dad.

Like they had at the bar, her tears had fallen unabated as she thought about how much she'd regretted not getting to see him before his death. Her sisters had come in at that moment, causing her to wipe her tears as they thought about what they needed to do.

"I'll stay," Cora had volunteered. "I don't really have anything to get back to in Seattle. I'm on a year-long leave from the paper, the girls are off doing their own thing and I am free..." She hadn't finished her statement, but her sisters were able to fill in the missing piece.

"Mom needs at least one of us to be here, so I'll do it," she finished.

Andrea and Josephine each gave her arm a gentle squeeze of gratitude and encouragement.

"I wish there was more I could do, but my job as a sous chef is too demanding. They wouldn't understand, and they would probably write it off as me abandoning my job. As soon as I get some things in order, I promise I'll do more," Andrea heard Josephine say.

"It's okay, Jo, I know. We'll make it work," Cora assured her.

"I promise, I'll be back by next week," Andrea spoke to Cora.

That had been over a month ago.

After fifteen minutes of traveling on the highway, she could see the Deception Pass Bridge. Even being a few feet away from its entrance, Andrea couldn't help but marvel at its magnificence. It was a remarkable structure, a complete wrought iron network that arched over the blue-green waters that were as tumultuous as they were deep. Yet, just looking over the drop-off, you couldn't help but be bowled over by the serenity of the view. There the welcomed view of the magnificent species of broad-winged birds hovering in the distance as the wind aided their seeming immobility, appearing transfixed in the air and the different landforms like small islands and wide mountain ranges that rose from the surface of the ocean. It all created the perfect, picture-worthy backdrop.

She remembered that on the north side of the bridge, you got the best views of the entire eastward side of Skagit County, and if you wanted, you could walk along the west side of the bridge and be blessed with a panoramic view of the Canadian border.

Just entering the bridge brought back so many memories of her time here on Whidbey Island. Those had been the best years of her life before life became complicated. Her heart raced in anticipation as she drove along the full length of the 453-foot bridge.

She was back. Back in Whidbey, on her way to Oak Harbor and her home. Andrea felt as if a hand was gripping her heart and squeezing it until it became almost unbearable to breathe. Even though she'd been back for the funeral, it felt as if it was the first time she was seeing the place in twenty-five years. When she'd attended her father's funeral, she had little time to focus on anything else.

Soon she passed the sign that read, "Welcome to Whidbey Island," displaying the most prominent activities that the island was popular for.

The view of the Cascade Mountain range with its snow-topped mountains came into view. It became the prominent feature in her mirror the further inland she drove.

As she traveled along the main road, she marveled at the way the overall layout remained the same despite a few new establishments she guessed sprang up after she left. The most drastic changes were found in Downtown Oak Harbor where it seemed a bit more urbanized than she remembered. There were a few high-rise business complexes, fast food restaurants, fine dining restaurants, and parking lots. Many of the single retail shops were still present, however. She was happy the town had managed to preserve its individuality.

Shortly after passing through the business district, Andrea made a turn onto NE 8th Ave when there was a sudden loud pop, and the car swerved to the side. Andrea quickly pumped the brakes, causing the Jeep to jolt to a stop. She slid out of the vehicle to inspect the damage.

"Shoot!" she exclaimed as she stared at the busted-up back wheel of the Jeep. There was no way she would make it to the property on a flat. She'd ruin the rim. The best she could do was probably try to make it to the old gas station that also housed a garage less than a mile away. At least she hoped it was still there. She remembered the owner Mr. Gourdie had been good friends with her father.

Andrea drove slowly, wincing every time the metal rim scraped against the asphalt.

"Please still be there," she whispered desperately.

Ten minutes later, she was pulling into the old gas station that looked as if it had seen better days. She was just happy it was still there. She pulled past the pumps and came to a stop at the small garage at the side.

An older man looking to be in his seventies stepped out in grease-stained overalls, looking at her vehicle with curiosity.

"Mr. Gourdie, it's Andrea Hamilton, Samuel Hamilton's—"

"Oh, you're one of old Sam's girls," the man interrupted.

Andrea gave him a sheepish smile.

"It's a real shame what happened to your father, you know. I'm really sorry for your loss. We were drinking buddies by the old pub on Regatta up until his passing."

Andrea shook her head in acknowledgment to the fast-talking man before her.

"So, what can I do for you?" he asked.

"Oh, my tire burst, and I didn't have a spare or the tools to remove it."

"Let's take a look then."

After inspecting the damage, Mr. Gourdie gave her an estimated cost before informing her it wouldn't be ready before the following day. Andrea grimaced to herself as she dug out her phone.

"Hi, Cora, it's Andrea. I'm at Mr. Gourdie's garage. My tire blew out. Can you come to get me?

Andrea leaned up against the building and out of the sun. She just hoped that the rest of the day went by uneventfully.

Chapter Four

Andrea watched as her sister's olive-green Range Rover pulled up to the gas station, a wide grin playing on her lips.

"Hey, Sis," she greeted with a smile of her own as soon as the vehicle stopped.

The two hugged before pulling away from each other.

"What on earth did you do for the tire to look like this?" Cora walked around the Jeep, inspecting the damage.

"It looks like a tired soufflé," she finished, snickering. "Get it? 'Tired' soufflé?"

Andrea shook her head while rolling her eyes at her sister's corny joke.

"That's not funny, Cora," she deadpanned.

This only seemed to fuel her sister's mirth, who was now bent over with her arms around her chest as uncontrollable laughter left her lips.

As bad as the joke was, her sister's laughter seemed to trigger something in her that caused her to chuckle.

"You're hopeless," she spat in between chuckles.

"At least I got you to you laugh. You should have seen your face earlier. It resembled the time when you couldn't find the camera Mom had bought you back in elementary school, and you went around moping till we all had to help you look for it."

Andrea was surprised by her sister's observation. She hadn't realized that she was projecting her inner turmoil. She was usually so stoic and only ever tried to appear good-humored no matter what was happening on the inside.

"I know it must have been hard on you these past few months since Dad's death. Believe me, it's been hard on me, too, especially with Mom's illness and all, but I want you to know that I'm here for you if you want to talk. I want to be there for you," Cora invited when Andrea didn't readily respond.

"Thanks, Cora," she replied gratefully.

Cora gave her a comforting smile before looking behind her once more.

"So, where's the luggage?" she asked.

"In the back of the Jeep," Andrea said, making her way over to the vehicle. She opened the back door and lifted out her suitcase, heavy with the clothes she'd packed. Cora came up and took it from her as she dipped back into the vehicle for the other carry-on roller bag that held her cameras and other vlogging equipment.

"Wow, this is really heavy," she heard Cora grunt from behind her.

"Just roll it on the wheels," she instructed.

"So, how long do you plan to stay?" Cora turned to ask after stuffing the suitcase in the back of her car.

"I'm still working that out in my head," she replied truthfully. "I'm not leaving anytime soon, though. My work is flexible enough so it can be done anywhere. Plus, I'm planning on cutting back on the number of clients I have too."

After giving Mr. Gourdie her contact number, the two left

for the place she once called her home— the place that would once again be her home for at least a month.

After a few minutes of driving in silence, Andrea asked, "How's Mom?"

"She's good, staying strong." Cora's hands tightened slightly on the wheel as she continued to stare ahead.

Andrea waited for her to continue.

"They switched out her medication last week, and since then, she has been sleeping a whole lot."

"So what are the doctors saying?" she asked, preparing herself for whatever news she was about to hear.

Cora sighed as she turned onto NE Regatta Dr. After a few more minutes of ensuing silence, she continued. "He said she's one of the lucky few because there are some new experimental drugs on the market that may possibly be able to help slow the rate of neuron deterioration. It's still on the table, though. No guarantees at all."

Andrea sighed, troubled by the uninspiring news. Even if their mother received the experimental drugs, the rate at which the drugs would slow down the progress of her disease would not be significant enough. At most, she probably had a few months to a year tops.

"We're just trying to take it one step at a time. You being here, I'm sure, will boost her spirit even more."

Andrea turned her head to see her sister staring back at her, a small encouraging smile on her lips. She returned the smile, but, on the inside, she was filled with angst.

When they finally made it onto Torpedo Road, which indicated that they were only a few minutes away from the driveway that led to the property, Andrea's heartbeat threatened to burst through her rib cage, and her stomach felt as if it was twisted in knots. Her knuckles lost all color as they tightly gripped the seat belt to keep them from shaking.

Andrea tried to take deep, slow breaths to reduce the

tension that was causing the nerve at her temple to pulsate the way it was. It was on the tip of her tongue to tell Cora to turn the car around and drive her back to Mr. Gourdie. She would wait on him to fix her tire and then return to her home in Arlington, where she had control over the events of her life. Maybe if she did, then that would mean all this wasn't real, that maybe it was just a figment of her imagination, and her father hadn't truly died a month ago, and her mother didn't have ALS.

She saw the upcoming turn on the left, a few feet away, and her heart slammed against her chest, squeezing out the last of her breath. Cora, as if sensing her unease, gave the hand in her lap a gentle squeeze, reminding Andrea that she was there for her. Andrea returned her sister's squeeze as she made the turn onto the semi-paved path and continued past the sign, "Welcome to Willberry Inn, Restaurant and Property."

As soon as they passed the semi-arched driveway, she took the time to admire the landscape. Even though she was only getting glimpses as Cora drove by, it could not be denied that the property looked even more spectacular than it had when she left. The lawn on either side of the path hedged by a plethora of colorful flowers and ornamentals was lusciously green and only interrupted by the Garry oak trees and caged by the thick woodlands that blocked the view of the Crescent Harbor— an extension of the whole property.

They passed the three-story colonial home that had been remodeled into an inn. It was just as she remembered it except for a few remodeling changes, such as the wide sliding windows and the wide balconies that surrounded the two upper floors. It was an all-white regal building accentuated by the large mahogany door with brass handles. Shortly after passing the inn, they drove by the new and improved barn house that had been remodeled and modernized into a restaurant. It still, however, maintained a rustic look with its natural stained wood exterior on display. Andrea appreciated the work and thought how much work had gone into it all.

Less than two minutes after, they pulled up to the house that held so many childhood memories of her. She braced herself for the onslaught of emotions like the first time they had bowled her over when she'd returned for her father's funeral.

"Everyone's around the back by the patio," Cora informed her as soon as they got out of the car.

"Okay, let me take my things to the room, freshen up a bit, and then I'll join the festivities." Andrea removed her luggage from the back of the car when the front door opened, causing her to look back. The man standing on the porch had such an uncanny resemblance to her father. Her heart lurched. She caught herself before the word "Daddy" left her mouth.

Uncle Luke walked over to them wearing a wide grin.

"Hey, kiddo, it's good to see you again."

Andrea walked into her uncle's waiting arms, hugging him tightly.

"It's good to be home, Uncle Luke." She sighed, drawing comfort and strength from the hulking man whose six-foot-three frame towered over her. His sandalwood scent was so reminiscent of her father's.

"Here, let me take those for you girls." Uncle Luke took hold of the suitcase and equipment bag and started for the porch. The sisters followed behind.

Andrea marveled at how easily he lifted the bags onto the porch without so much as a hint of strain. At seventy-six, her uncle was still as sturdy as he had been in his younger years.

As soon as she stepped through the front door and into the foyer, memories of her childhood played rapidly through her mind. She remembered the round mahogany center table that still held the ceramic vase that she'd broken by accident. A small smile graced her lips as she recalled how she and her sisters had frantically tried to glue the pieces back together before their parents could have seen it. Unfortunately, they had not done such a great job, and some of the colored pieces had been misplaced. It took no time for her parents to see the poorly done job. Her sisters had stuck up for her by implicating themselves in the act. Her heart skipped a beat, and she was reminded of how it was now.

A wave of nostalgia hit her, and she yearned for the happy family they had been so long ago before everything changed. Perhaps being here now could be a way to rebuild the bond with her entire family.

Uncle Luke set her luggage down in front of her old bedroom before turning to them.

"I'm gonna head on out to the backyard. I left my grandson Trevor to watch over the grill, but you know how these young ones are, always distracted. He's always on that smartphone doing what only God knows. I'm gonna go rescue our food, so we don't have to eat charred meat."

Andrea laughed at the face her uncle made as if he imagined the awful taste of the meat if he allowed his grandson to take over.

"I'll see you girls outside."

"Thanks again, Uncle Luke." Andrea gave him a quick hug before he turned and walked off.

Her room looked the same as she'd left it twenty-five years ago. Her Bruce Springsteen and Queen larger-than-life posters still hung across from each other on opposite walls. A poster of Rob Lowe, her celebrity crush back in the day, stood over her double bed that was adorned with the colorful patchwork quilt she'd gotten as a gift from her aunt Stacey on her fifteenth birthday. Her study desk was still in one of the far corners with books from high school, and her trophies from various academic and sports achievements still featured prominently from the wall shelves and on the top of her chest of drawers.

Andrea ran her hands over the memorabilia that were a

reminder of how her life was when she was a teenager. It brought a small smile to her lips.

"It brings back memories, doesn't it?" Cora stood by the door, watching her sister reacquaint herself with her room.

"It does." She released a sigh.

"I'll see you down there. I'll give you some time to yourself." The door closed with a soft click.

Andrea walked over to her bed, sat, and exhaled the breath she'd been holding. She knew she needed to go down shortly, but she was happy for the few minutes by herself.

Ten minutes later, Andrea walked out of her room and made her way down the stairs. She walked to the back door that led to the back porch and opened it.

The view before her was spectacular.

Chapter Five

Andrea was greeted by the sound of loud chatter and laughing as soon as she stepped through the porch door.

There had to be more than fifteen of her family members out by the patio, some she was able to recognize and some not so well.

Making her way off the back porch, she made the short walk toward the gathering.

"There you are." Cora was the first one to spot her.

She'd been standing by the patio entrance speaking with another woman who looked about their age. When Cora acknowledged her presence, the woman turned in her direction, a small smile of recognition on her lips. She looked very familiar. As soon as she focused on the electric blue eyes that were so compelling and made you feel as if they were staring straight into your soul, coupled with the chestnut-colored hair, she knew who it was.

"Tessa," she found herself saying in wonder.

"Oh my God, Andrea. It's been too long." The woman

walked over to her and, without hesitation, wrapped her arms around Andrea's shoulders.

"I'm sorry I didn't make it back in time for Uncle Sam's funeral, but I'm so happy to see you." Pulling away from Tessa, Andrea gave her arm a short squeeze.

"It's so nice to see you, too, Tessa," she replied sincerely.

Cora, who had remained silent, watching the interaction, walked up to them.

"The others are waiting to greet you," she informed her. Andrea turned to see that most of the people who had been chatting and laughing a short while ago were staring in her direction.

She felt self-conscious. Even though she'd briefly spoken to a few of her cousins and their children at the funeral, she still didn't know them that well, but if they were willing to come and be a part of the family gathering, then she supposed that meant they had an interest in rebuilding the family bond.

As she walked toward them, she took the time to look over the patio space. She remembered her mother explaining that her father had hired Jamie Hillier to make it a few years back so they could host family gatherings like this one.

She liked the space, especially the irregular mosaic flag-stones that lined the floor and the semi-circular enclosure stone wall that provided additional seating if the bamboo chairs or the long stone bench on either side of the stone table wasn't adequate. She also loved how the colored cushions comple-mented the floor. It all reminded her of the last few days of fall when the trees were down to their last set of leaves, getting ready to fall to join the ones on the ground that had started to lose their bright color.

She especially liked the view it provided of the harbor, where the trees that lined most of the property's border thinned to reveal the pristine waters reflecting the blue of the sky. From this distance, she could see a few sailboats on the horizon. It was so beautiful.

Andrea noted the charcoal barrel grill and smoker in one corner where Uncle Luke stood flipping what looked like steaks.

She could envision herself standing by that same grill flipping steaks or maybe some burgers before her family, who would be happily lounging around and enjoying themselves— her father included. She pushed the thought away as another of her cousins greeted her. This time it was Uncle Luke's son Charles.

"Andrea, it's great to see you again."

"It's good to see you again too, Charlie," she greeted him by the old childhood nickname.

"You already met Sharon." He gestured to the small brunette standing at his side.

"Yes. It's nice to see you again, Sharon," she acknowledged.

The woman gave her a warm smile as she shook her hand.

"And this is Trevor, our youngest." Andrea looked at the young man, who seemed to be in his early twenties sitting on the stone bench before the table.

Trevor barely turned his eyes toward her and gave a slight nod of greeting before his eyes were once again focused on whatever was on his screen.

She heard Charles's sigh of frustration at his son's lack of interest but knew it would be a lost cause to prolong any interaction with him. Trevor then continued to introduce a young woman that had shiny black hair cut in a sleek bob just below her chin.

"This is our daughter Sara. She works with Sharon and I at the law firm."

"Hi, Sara. It's a pleasure to meet you." Andrea gave the young woman a bright, inviting smile, which she returned, her light caramel eyes shining.

"It's a pleasure to meet you too."

Charles expressed that his daughter Cassidy was away at John Hopkins University studying neuroscience. She could hear the pride with which he spoke about his two girls, but she could also see how irritated Trevor was as she caught him rolling his eyes at one point in Charles's introduction.

Andrea spent the next twenty minutes being reintroduced to the rest of her family.

She met Tessa's children, Diane, who owned a coffee shop called the Java Bistro in town, and Jake, a graphic designer.

She also met her cousin Kerry who was a divorcee, along with her two children, Tracy and Emma. Uncle Luke's other son Brian hadn't made it, but his daughter Nikki came. She worked at her aunt Kerry's bakery, Heavenly Treats.

Aunt Stacy's daughter Rhonda was also there with her husband Shawn and their daughter Natalie. The number was incomplete, but she was happy to see so many of her family together again. It was hard to remember them all, along with all their names.

It brought back memories of when they used to have these get-togethers in the backyard and how she and her cousins would entertain themselves with various sporting activities while the adults were preoccupied. Those had been some great times. There were so many great memories.

Even though their children were a lot older than they were, she hoped that they could possibly have the chance to have a bond like they had in the past.

"Where's Mom?" Andrea asked, looking around the gathering but not seeing her mother anywhere.

"She went to give Marg a plate from the barbecue," Cora replied.

Andrea remembered Marg was the receptionist at the inn. From the brief introduction they had, she could tell that the woman had a very likable personality.

"Hey, kiddo, come over here and let me show you something." Andrea looked toward her uncle, who used the tongs in his hand to beckon her. She excused herself and walked over to him.

"Uncle Luke, don't you think it's time that name got retired? I'm far from being a kid."

Uncle Luke gave her a mischievous smile. "You will always be kiddo to me, kid." He smirked.

Andrea playfully rolled her eyes as she went to stand at his side by the grill.

"I got this for you, but I didn't want to start a riot by giving it to you in front of everyone. I remembered how you used to love these things."

Andrea looked down to see her uncle holding out a small gold box for her to take.

"This isn't what I think it is?" she asked, barely able to contain her excitement.

"Why don't you open it to find out?" he told her.

Andrea turned toward the grill and carefully lifted the box cover to confirm what she thought.

Tucked neatly into individual sections were six chocolate truffles, her favorite and only guilty pleasure.

"Oh my gosh. Thanks, Uncle Luke." Reaching her right arm over, she gave him a side hug.

"Anytime, kiddo," he returned, patting the arm around his shoulder. This time she didn't protest about still being called by her old nickname.

She discretely placed the box into the side of her jacket before walking over to her sister and cousins to continue conversing.

"Andrea, sweetie, you're here."

Andrea turned to see her mother smiling at her, relief reflecting in her light brown eyes.

"Hi, Mom." Andrea walked over and gave her mother a light kiss on the cheek as she embraced her.

"So, are you only staying a few days again?" Becky asked her daughter as they made their way to sit in the two unoccupied wicker chairs in the corner.

"Actually, Mom, I decided to stay and help Cora with everything. So, I'll be here a while," she informed her mother.

"You don't have to do that, sweetie. I know how busy you must be with your work and all."

"Mom," Andrea stopped her mother. "It's fine. I want to be here for you and for Cora. I know she needs the help. Besides, I can work from anywhere, so it's fine," she reasoned.

"In that case, I'm happy you're here." Becky beamed, but she could still see the apprehension in her eyes.

A few minutes into sitting and catching up, they were called to get their plates. Everyone sat at the long table that still had space to hold more than the nineteen people currently seated there.

"So, how is my beautiful granddaughter doing?" Becky asked her as conversation flowed around the table.

"Rory is a great, Mom." A broad graced her lips as she thought about her daughter.

"She just got engaged," she broke the news.

"That's wonderful news, sweetie," her mother congratulated.

"Yes, I'm really excited for her and James."

The rest of the family offered their congratulations as they all ate heartedly.

"So will the wedding be held here?" her cousin Kerry who sat two seats away, asked.

"Oh, no, she wanted to keep it in San Francisco. She already booked the venue for the reception," she explained.

"Well, if she changes her mind and decides to have it here, I would be more than happy to bake her wedding cake, free of charge," she offered.

"Thank you, Kerry. I'm sure she would appreciate the gesture." Andrea gave her cousin a smile of gratitude.

"You know that isn't a bad idea. Oak Harbor would be a wonderful place for her to have her wedding. There are so many different spots on the property that would make for the perfect backdrop for her nuptials," her mother chimed in, already sold on the idea.

"Maybe you should ask her and see if she agrees," Cora told her.

Andrea considered the suggestions her family made and decided it wasn't a bad idea. There were so many places that she'd identified for the perfect wedding setup, like down by the docks, and the gazebo built behind the inn that Cora had sent pictures of to her. There was also the rose garden that she'd gotten a brief glimpse of when she'd been there a month back. There was nowhere on the property that wouldn't be a good choice for the wedding and the reception.

"Now that I think about it, you're all right. This is the perfect place to have a wedding or even the reception. It's a dream destination," she agreed.

After she filled her plate for seconds and complimented Uncle Luke on his prowess in using the grill to turn out the best outdoor meal she'd had in a while, the family sat sipping wine, at least those who were old enough to or those who weren't on medication. The conversations were light and entertaining, and Andrea found herself laughing nonstop.

When Cora rose to move the dishes inside, she got up to help her. The other females offered their help, but they assured them that they had it under control. While Cora washed, Andrea rinsed and dried the dishes, resting them on the counter.

"I thought after all these years being apart from our family would have made it really weird for us to come together like this. I had my doubts, but I'm glad you guys chose to have this barbecue," Andrea broke the silence they'd been working in.

Cora looked over at her sister and gave her an encouraging smile.

"They have been great," she confessed, referring to her cousins. "They've been coming by regularly just to catch up or just to drop off food. I was just as surprised as you, but I've come to appreciate their support."

Andrea felt a pair of hands wrap around her torso as Cora pulled her to her side and rested her cheek on her shoulder.

"I'm really sorry I wasn't there for you all those years ago, Drea." She sighed sadly. "If I could reverse time, I would have done things so differently."

Andrea felt her eyes dampen at the sincerity coming from her sister.

"I missed you, Cora." Her voice broke with her vulnerability.

"I missed you too, Drea. I'm sorry for not being there, but I want to be there for you now."

Just then, their mother walked in, freezing at the scene before her.

"Your father would be so happy to see you both here in this manner," she spoke with such emotion. Going over to her daughters, she engulfed both of them.

The three of them stood there, not letting each go, when Becky finally murmured, "I'm so happy you're finally home. My girls are home."

Chapter Six

Andrea's eyes fluttered open as the bright light streaming through the window cast shadows on her closed lids. Raising herself into a sitting position, she stared at her opened window, no longer obscured by the thick satin blue curtains but instead had invited the warm gold hue of the risen sun that bathed everything in the room it touched with its brightness.

Rising from the bed, she stretched away some of the tiredness. Heading over to the vanity, she stared at her reflection in the mirror. She still looked as if she could use a couple more hours of sleep, but the subtle invitation that the sun and the chirping birds gave her made her feel like if she didn't end up outside shortly, she would regret it.

Reaching for her toiletries and a towel, she made her way to the bathroom across the hall from her room. This was the bathroom she'd shared with her two sisters when they were growing up. Even though there was an extra bathroom on the floor, it had been reserved for any guests that stayed at the house. Their parents would not budge in letting them use both bathrooms.

They had said it was to teach them proper time management and to care about each other's feelings.

Now, as she went to open the door, out of habit, she stared at the knob to ensure nothing wasn't hanging around it, as that was usually the way they knew when one of the sisters was in the bathroom. Andrea shook her head as she pulled the door open and entered the bathroom to take a shower and get ready for the day.

Once dressed, she could smell the aroma of freshly brewed coffee wafting up to her before she'd fully descended the stairs. No one was in the kitchen when she entered, but a plate of mouth-watering cinnamon rolls wrapped in saran plastic was sitting on the kitchen island while the fresh dark liquid dripped into the coffee pot. The rich, heady aroma of the coffee, mixed with the warm cinnamon scent of the pastries, was an inviting combo. There was no way she could pass up on having a cup and taking a bite out of one of the fresh rolls.

Andrea reached into the cupboard for a mug before walking over to the coffee maker. She poured the black liquid into the mug before replacing the receptacle under the still-dripping filter. She then moved to the refrigerator to get the cream. She poured a liberal amount into her coffee before adding a spoonful of sugar and stirring it. She took a cinnamon roll from the plate before resting her back against the counter and enjoying the quietness of her surroundings.

She took a few sips of the coffee, the bittersweet taste of the beverage, the cream lightening the bitterness. As she sipped, she thought about the things she needed to get done, like setting up a space to work on her social media content and running her client's ads. She would have to ask her mother or Cora if they would mind her paying for a room at the inn to do so.

Placing the mug on the counter, she took a bite of the roll, closing her eyes and indulging in the guilty pleasure. It was fluffy, cinnamon-infused, sweet dough that left a buttery aftertaste on her tongue. Just then, she opened her eyes to catch movement out the window above the kitchen sink. She looked over at the window and saw another slight movement. Andrea walked over to the window and peered out to see her sister on the porch swing, moving back and forth slowly as she looked ahead of her while she cradled a mug in her hand. Andrea grabbed her own mug and made her way outside to join her sister.

"Good morning." Andrea sat on the other end of the bench as it continued to move back and forth. Cora turned her head to look at her.

"Good morning to you," she returned with a smile on her lips.

The two sat in silence for a while, neither feeling the need to speak but rather enjoying each other's company while enjoying the beauty before them.

"So, how does it feel to be back here?" Cora finally asked.

Andrea looked out at the wide expanse of their property, contemplating how to answer her sister's question.

"It feels good to be back, but at the same time, it feels unreal with Dad being gone and Mom being sick and all," she answered truthfully.

She brought the mug back to her lips and took another sip of the drink that was giving her life.

"I feel like I'm finally getting back my family, but..." She paused, not sure how to finish her statement. "I feel guilty for not coming back before...before it was too late." Andrea sighed, running a hand over her face.

Cora looked over at her in understanding. "I know how you feel," she admitted. "But we're here now. Let's just try taking it one day at a time and try to fix what we can fix now— like our relationship," she encouraged.

"Okay," Andrea agreed, turning to look out at the harbor

that wasn't obscured by trees on that side of the wraparound porch.

"It's so serene here," she voiced her admiration.

"Hmm," was Cora's reply.

"I could definitely see myself in a wedding here," she continued dreamily.

This caused Cora's head to snap toward her.

"Don't tell me you've been holding out on me like that."

The mock hurt in Cora's voice caused her to turn her head toward her sister, perplexed. "What do you mean?" she asked, straightening up to look at her.

"When are you going to introduce us to this mystery man that has you thinking about weddings?" she asked with a mischievous glint in her eyes.

"What! No!" Andrea exclaimed. "I was just thinking about Aurora and imagining the possibilities of her having her wedding here," she corrected her sister's assumptions.

"So, you're not seeing anyone?" Cora asked, still curious about her sister's love life.

"I'm not seeing anyone. I don't have time to be in a relationship with anyone. I've been fine by myself all these years. There's no sense complicating what has been working for me for so long," she rationalized.

Cora gave her a sympathetic smile. "Drea—"

"Cora, it's fine. Can we just drop it for now?" she pleaded.

She didn't want to talk about her love life or the lack thereof. How could she explain to anyone that she was afraid to take a risk on loving someone and getting her heart broken when everyone saw her as a fearless person who took all the chances in life? All these years, and she was still tainted by what happened to her.

"Besides, I'm more interested in your friendship with that fine specimen of a man," she remarked, turning the tables on her sister. "How is Jamie, by the way?"

A rosy tint crept into Cora's cheeks at the mention of the handsome contractor that had been steadily wooing her since she sorted through her divorce from her cheating husband.

"Jamie is fine."

Andrea smirked at her sister's coquettish behavior. She could tell that her sister really liked Jamie, even though she was aware that she also had reservations about getting into a relationship with him after what happened with her ex.

"We're...we're just friends, Drea. We're spending the time to get to know each other better. He's been understanding, and I really appreciate him for that."

This brought a genuine smile of happiness to Andrea's lips. She was happy that her sister was able to find someone that would treat her with respect, and from what she was told, it was definitely her opinion that Jamie already worshipped the ground her sister walked on, even if they were just friends as her sister kept stressing.

"Last week, I went with him to visit the grave of his late wife. He brought her favorite flowers, and he cleaned her headstone. Then he introduced me as someone special."

Andrea could see the twinkle in her sister's blue-gray eyes become brighter the more she spoke about Jamie. "What happened to his wife?" she asked out of curiosity.

"She had leukemia. When they detected it, it was too aggressive to be treated effectively, and she died within a year of being diagnosed," Cora explained.

"Oh my God. I can't even imagine going through something like that. Poor Jamie." Andrea truly felt sad for the gentleman she'd seen only two times in person.

"They all took it hard, especially his daughter. His wife was a strong woman, though. He said she wasn't afraid to die, but she was worried that he would stop living his life, and she didn't want that for him. He promised her he would continue living."

The two sat in comfortable silence once more, finishing off the remains of their now lukewarm coffee and looking out across the property.

Cora was the first to break the silence once more. "So, you didn't tell me how your event went."

"It was great. All my worry and anxiety paid off in the end," she explained.

"That's good. I'm happy for you, Drea. No one deserves to be as successful as you do," her sister congratulated.

Andrea looked over and gave her a grateful smile.

"I was thinking about going down to the dock. Care to join me?" Cora was now standing over her with an expectant look.

"Yes, I would. I haven't seen that dock in ages." Andrea rose from the swing as she spoke.

"It hasn't changed that much, but there are a few surprises," Cora stated.

After rinsing out their mugs and replacing them in the cupboard, the two girls made their way to the back porch.

Andrea followed closely behind Cora, enjoying the scenic view. The paved pathway led them alongside the rose garden that, even from the outside, looked like a haven. She made a mental note to visit it soon.

When they cleared the thick forest of trees, they were finally blessed by the beautiful evergreen mountain range covered in a coat of snow at the top of its peak. It rose regally from the blue-green waters as the sun cast the perfect amount of light on the water's surface, causing the range to cast its own shadow on the waters. There were a few sailboats and fishing vessels gliding along the surface of the water.

Cora headed toward the dock, and that's when Andrea recognized the work being done there. From what she could see, a second platform was being added to the dock.

"Dad commissioned Jamie to make the dock a double-decker so that the boat can be moored under the bottom," Cora explained as her sister followed her.

When they finally made it atop the lower deck of the dock, Andrea was greeted by the shiny new boat underneath. It had the words *Silver Bullet* written stylishly across the side.

"Dad had Jamie restore and rename it."

Andrea looked over at Cora in disbelief. "You're telling me this is the old boat?" she asked, taking a step closer.

Cora nodded in agreement.

Andrea ran her hand over the varnish of the boat, tracing the letters. She knew the significance of the name. It confirmed to her that their father truly had been making preparations to make amends with them. She felt a tear run down her cheek at the sentimental value this one gesture held.

Andrea turned to her sister then. "What do you need help with, Cora? Tell me. I'll do anything. If it's to prepare the meals, take Mom to her appointments, or clean the inn, I'll do it," she said with so much emotion. In this instance, she wanted to do as much as she could to honor the memory of her father and for the rebuilding of her family.

"Let's take it one step at a time." Cora gave her hand a grateful squeeze. "I'm just happy you're here."

Andrea's phone rang, interrupting what she was about to say. She pulled her phone from her back jean pocket and held the phone to her ear. "Hello?"

"Hello, this is Mr. Gourdie from the garage. I just wanted you to know you can pick up your Jeep. it's finished."

Chapter Seven

"**H**ave you got your license?"

Andrea looked over at her sister, who was staring at her pointedly.

"Yes, I do. It never leaves my purse." She opened the flap of her slim MK purse to reveal her license in one of the pockets in the lining.

"Good," Cora replied with a smile.

"Good," she repeated with a smile of her own. Opening the door, she stepped out of the car before closing it.

"I'll see you back at home. I have a few things to take care of in town," Cora said as she peered through the window at her.

"Bye, Sis."

Cora pulled out of the gas station, and Andrea watched the SUV make its way down the street until it disappeared. She turned and drove toward Mr. Gourdie, who was perched on a stool on the outside of the garage, watching her approach.

"Hi, Mr. Gourdie. Thank you so much for working so quickly on my Jeep," she said.

"It wasn't that much trouble," he informed her as he slid off the stool to stand before her.

"How much do I owe you for this?" Andrea opened her purse, getting ready to take out the number of bills needed to pay for the new tire and labor that was put into her Jeep.

"That'll be one hundred and fifty dollars."

Andrea took the bills from her purse and handed them to the gentleman.

A voice rang out in the distance. "Drea, is that you?"

Andrea turned to see a woman that looked to be about her age looking at her in surprise. She looked vaguely familiar, but Andrea couldn't be sure how she knew her. Her brown ombre shoulder-length hair was swept away from her oval face, which was sporting a huge grin.

The closer she got to Andrea, the more recognizable she became.

"Shelby," Andrea greeted the woman who was now only a few inches from her. She was relieved that she'd recognized her in time as she couldn't bear the awkwardness of having to ask the woman to remind her who she was.

As soon as Shelby was close enough, the two embraced like two long-lost friends who had finally gotten the opportunity to reunite.

"It's so good to see you, Drea," Shelby spoke cheerily as they pulled apart.

"It has been too long," Andrea responded.

Shelby Dawson had been one of her good friends in high school.

"I heard you had been back for your father's funeral. I'm really sorry about what happened, Drea. How are you coping?" Shelby gave her a sympathetic look.

"It's okay. We're getting through it," she replied with a small smile of reassurance to her old friend.

"So, how long are you staying? Or are you heading out?" Shelby enquired.

"I'm not. I'm staying here for a while," she informed Shelby. "I just came to pick up my Jeep— the tire blew out, and I didn't have a spare," she explained.

"Oh, that's great. That means we can spend some time catching up," Shelby expressed excitedly. "There's so much I want to tell you."

Andrea cracked a smile at the woman's enthusiasm. It should have been an awkward meeting with them not seeing each other for nearly a quarter of a century. Yet, here was her old friend wanting them to spend time together.

"I can't wait to tell Randy that you're back."

"You mean Randy Barrett? He's still here in Oak Harbor?"

Shelby gave Andrea a weird look which made her regret asking that question.

"Yes, of course. I married him. He's my husband."

Andrea was bowled over by her friend's revelation. The last time she'd seen Randy, he was leaving on the ferry for Seattle. He was flying out to go backpacking across Europe for a year. After that, he would take up his deferred space at Princeton.

Even though he had been a year older than them, they had all been friends since elementary school. He was one of her friends who had vowed that when he left Oak Harbor, he wouldn't be returning to live.

"It's a lot to take in, I know," Shelby cut into her thoughts.

"I'm sorry, Shelby. It's just that I remember Randy was one of the persons in our group who was adamant to never return," she tried to explain.

Shelby smiled, nodding in understanding.

"You would be surprised to know how many of those people are back here in Oak Harbor."

Andrea was surprised at the revelation.

"Tell you what; why don't we grab a cup of coffee now, and

I can catch you up on all that has happened in your absence. That's if you're not busy."

Andrea smiled, delighted by the gesture. "I would love that," she agreed. "Why don't we go by my family's restaurant?"

"Sure. Why not? Let me just go get my car. Mr. Gourdie called me in to pick it up."

The two women made their way to the old man, who was once again perched on the bench by the garage's entrance. Andrea thanked him again for helping and went by her Jeep to wait for Shelby.

She saw the woman walk toward her, a look of displeasure etched on her face. She wondered what could have transpired to transform her features so drastically.

"What's wrong?" she asked out of concern.

Shelby released a frustrated sigh. "Gourdie says my car isn't ready. He explained the battery needs to be changed, and if he lets me leave with it, there is a high chance it will break down on me."

"Oh, that's tough."

"I'm sorry, Drea, maybe a rain check on that coffee. I'm gonna call Randy to come to pick me up."

Andrea watched the upset woman fish for her phone in her bag. She felt bad for her as she knew how debilitating it could feel to be without your car for any period of time.

"Why don't I take you to get that coffee, and then I can drive you back. It's not a problem at all, and it'll be great to catch up."

Shelby paused what she was doing to look up at Andrea, a mixture of shock and gratitude on her face. "That would be lovely," she agreed.

The two women got into Andrea's Jeep, and she drove them back to her family's property.

"This inn is a town treasure. I'm glad it's still here, you

know, considering how much outside developers have been trying to buy out all the properties along the harbor to throw up resorts. I feel like if that happens, and these monuments are destroyed, then most of everything that makes Oak Harbor special will be lost."

Andrea shook her head in agreement, staring up at the building.

"This inn is one of the oldest historical buildings in Oak Harbor; it was once the residence of the governor of the island in the nineteenth century before it was sold to a businessman who later sold it to your great-grandfather four times removed. My great-great-grandfather chose to turn it into an inn, and it has been passed down to the firstborn of each generation since, except your uncle Luke went away to fight in the war against our father's wishes, and so it passed on to me. Soon it will all be yours to build on and continue the legacy."

Andrea's father looked at his girls with pride and expectation as they all sat, nodding in agreement. At just twelve, ten, and eight, they had no idea of what they agreed to or the implications it would have for years to come.

"Drea, are you okay?"

Andrea blinked away the memory and turned her focus back to her friend.

"Oh, yes, I was just remembering something my father told me back when I was a kid."

Two minutes later, they were pulling up to the restaurant. The signboard attached to a wooden frame read, "Willberry Eats."

The women entered the rustic yet very modern-looking restaurant. The first thing Andrea noticed and truly appreciated was how large and airy the space was. The inside, like the outside, had a rustic feel with its stained wood interior, tables, and chairs. The high gambrel roof also lent to the rustic feel of the place, and she especially liked the low hanging lights on the far corners and ceiling fans in the middle of the rafter beams from front to back that added the right balance between rural and urban style. She also liked the fact that the restaurant could remain lit during the days just from the light streaming through the large glass windows all around the inn. Her father truly had been an artist in disguise. There was not one thing she hated about the design.

"Welcome to Willberry Eats, where we serve nothing but the best freshly caught seafood and a variety of five-star dishes. May I take you to your seats?"

Andrea smiled at the bubbly young waitress whose name tag read "Suzie."

"Thank you, Suzie. We'll take a seat close to the back," Andrea told her.

"Right this way, please."

The young woman took them to a seat in the back. Although it was not an inconspicuous spot, Andrea appreciated the level of privacy it provided as it was further away from the other tables.

"May I take your order?" the waitress asked, removing a notepad with an attached pen from her side.

"I'll just have a coffee," she informed her.

"Me as well," Shelby jumped in.

"Will that be with cream or without?"

Andrea looked up at the young woman, holding the pen expectantly over the notepad for her response. "With cream," she smiled.

When the waitress didn't make a move to go and get their order, Andrea raised her head to see the young woman looking at her curiously— as if she were a puzzle that needed to be solved.

"I'll go get your order," she said quickly after being caught.

When she disappeared, Andrea turned her head back to her friend, who was also staring at her in curiosity.

"I take it they don't know who you are," Shelby spoke, questioning.

"Not really," she confirmed. "They might have seen me when I came to my father's funeral, but that's just about it."

"It seems that young lady recognized you, judging by the way she kept staring at you," Shelby volunteered.

"Maybe." She shrugged. "So, you're married?"

"Yes, I sure am. Next month will make fifteen years since we tied the knot."

Just then, the waitress returned with their coffee, a small pitcher of cream, and a sugar shaker.

The two women thanked her before she left them.

"So, what do you do now?" Andrea took a sip of her coffee, waiting for Shelby's reply.

"Well, I'm a nurse, but I took some time off after I had my third child to spend more time with them," Shelby informed Andrea, taking a sip of her own coffee. After placing the cup back in the saucer, she delved into her bag, pulling out some pictures.

"This is Ricky, he's the oldest at fourteen; and Angela, she's twelve, and this is Isaac, he's seven."

Andrea gushed over the photos her friend was showing her of her kids. "They're beautiful, Shelby," she complimented.

"Thank you. Do you have kids of your own?"

At this, Andrea's face lit up with pride. "Yes. Her name is Aurora, or Rory for short." She opened up her purse to show Shelby a photo of her daughter.

"She's beautiful," Shelby expressed, causing an even wider smile to appear on Andrea's lips.

"She's my world."

"I know what you mean," Shelby agreed. "As much as my kids get on my nerves, I wouldn't trade them for the world."

Andrea raised her cup to toast the statement.

"Ms. Hamilton."

Andrea turned to see a short, stout man in a gray chef's jacket standing at their table. "How do you do?" he asked with a deep bow. He had a slight accent, Andrea noted.

"I am well, thank you for asking." Andrea couldn't recall ever meeting the man who stood before her beaming, and so she couldn't put a name to the face.

"I am Chef Daniel, but you can call me Chef."

Chapter Eight

"It is a pleasure to meet you, Chef." Andrea held out her hand to the gentleman before her, who eagerly grasped her hand.

"Please feel free to order anything you'd like. I would be more than happy to whip that up for you, Mademoiselle Hamilton."

Chef Daniel stood before the table with his hands behind his back and a welcoming smile that Andrea couldn't help but return.

"Thank you, Chef, I appreciate the offer, but it's just coffee for me today," she told him.

The man gave a slight nod of acknowledgment.

"What about you, Shelby? Would you like to order anything?" Andrea turned to her friend expectantly.

"That's okay, Drea. I don't want to spoil my appetite for later. We're actually going out for dinner, my family and I," Shelby informed her.

"But I would like another cup of coffee if that's not too much trouble." Shelby held up her empty cup.

"Of course, not a problem. I'll have our waitress Suzie bring it to you," Chef offered.

As they watched the chef retreat back to the kitchen, they sipped their coffee and carried on with their conversation.

"Wow, an oncologist, that's great, Shelby. You must be so proud of Randy for following his dreams," Andrea said sincerely. She remembered Randy had expressed his desire to become an oncologist, to help people. His sister had died from a rare kind of cancer that the oncology department of Whidbey Medical Hospital had failed to catch. By the time they had taken her to Seattle Grace for a second opinion, it had been too late.

"Yes." Shelby beamed with pride. "That's the reason he came back to Oak Harbor. He had a great job at the Mayo Clinic, but he said he couldn't shake the feeling that this was where God wanted him to be. Now, he's the head of oncology and finding innovative ways of treating cancer so that there are more survivors."

Andrea's eyes stayed focused on Shelby as she spoke. She couldn't deny how admirable Randy's actions were, and she realized that she was happy for them both. At first, she was shocked by the pairing as she remembered they weren't as close back in high school. If she remembered correctly, she and her sisters had been the glue that brought their group of friends together.

"So, I heard that you are a big shot social media guru. How does it feel being famous?"

Andrea chuckled. "I wouldn't say I'm that big of a star. I do ads for various companies, and I have a blog and a YouTube channel with a few thousand subscribers, but I am not insta famous," she replied meekly. "I do well for myself, though. So I can't complain."

"Oh, come on, Drea, you're being too modest," Shelby chided with a scowl.

Andrea laughed at her friend's actions, especially when she couldn't stay in character, and cracked a smile.

The two spent the next hour talking, and trading stories of their lives before Shelby indicated it was time for her to leave.

The journey to Shelby's home on Cathlamat Drive took half an hour. When they pulled up to the property, Andrea was impressed by the two-story brick home. "Your house is beautiful," she complimented.

"Thank you. Would you like to come in?" Shelby looked at her expectantly.

"No, not today. I need to get back," she informed her.

"Okay, no problem. It was really great seeing you today, Drea. I enjoyed your company."

Andrea smiled back at her friend. "It truly was, Shelby," she gladly agreed. "We should do this again soon."

"Sure, you have my number, and I have yours."

Andrea pulled out of Shelby's driveway as she waved goodbye.

It had been a surprise not only to see Shelby but to have spent time catching up as if there weren't twenty-four years of no contact. She wondered if meeting up with her other high school friends who had returned to Oak Harbor would be the same. She wondered if they would fall into a routine of catching up on each other's lives or if there would just be moments of uncomfortable silence and the need to end their meetup as quickly as possible. A lot had changed after all.

She wished she had the power to turn back time; she wished she'd kept in contact with at least a few of her friends, but after leaving Oak Harbor and falling on hard times, she felt too ashamed to be in contact with anyone from her past. They reminded her of all her dreams and aspirations. She hadn't wanted them to witness how much of a screwup she'd become, not after she'd been voted as one of the persons most likely to succeed after high school.

When she got pregnant with Rory and realized that she would have to do it all on her own, any ties she'd left to Oak Harbor were cut, and she threw herself into making a life for her and her daughter. Now here she was, a successful social media personality but with people around her who knew nothing about her. The friendships she had back in New York and when she moved to Arlington had all been superficial. In doing this, she never had to worry about losing anyone else in her life, and if at any one moment she needed to pack up and leave to start over somewhere else, she could without feeling any guilt.

Being back in Oak Harbor had shifted her perspective, though. Talking to Shelby today reminded her that along with her sisters, her friends had been just as important to her.

After being so lost in her own thoughts, Andrea found herself on NE 8th Avenue making her way toward NE Regatta Drive. She almost ran the red light but stopped just in the nick of time. At the same time, she heard a loud thump, and her car lurched forward, luckily not enough for her to be in the way of oncoming traffic.

Her heart slammed into her chest, and her palms became sweaty as she tried to breathe. Slowly she pulled the vehicle off the road and got out as she began to hyperventilate. Andrea put her hands on her thighs with her head down as she tried to take in long calming breaths.

"Are you all right, ma'am?" someone from above her asked, but she still couldn't breathe properly, so she didn't answer.

Putting her hand up to indicate to them to give her some time, she took in some more calming breaths before she looked up to meet the concerned blue eyes that stared back at her.

Finally, feeling strong enough to get herself in an upright position, she straightened herself. Andrea looked from the sandy blond-haired man before her to the navy blue SUV parked just behind her Jeep with a smidge of army green paint on one of the headlights before staring him down in anger.

"Are you out of your mind?" she asked, annoyance marring her face.

The man took a step back as if she'd slapped him.

After no reply, she continued. "You nearly ran me into the path of oncoming traffic. I could have been hit, and the impact could have killed me!" she screeched at him.

"What?" He looked completely perplexed by her words.

"Don't you pay attention to your surroundings?" Andrea couldn't stop herself from going off on the man that stood before her. He looked at her in disbelief. The fact that her father had died in a car accident was still fresh in her mind, and she'd been severely rattled that the same thing almost just happened to her.

"Lady, I don't see how you're blaming me right now when you stopped so abruptly on me. I tried to brake to prevent the accident, but it was already too late. How can you be blaming me when you made a sudden stop after driving at fifty miles per hour?" he asked, offended.

"You should be paying attention to the road! You shouldn't be driving so close to another car. Two car lengths is a safe distance, but no, you were almost tailgating me," she returned, equally rattled.

The man looked at her for a long time as if she'd grown two heads. Finally, he let out an exasperated sigh before muttering something under his breath.

Andrea hadn't heard what he said, but she caught the word "*dumb*."

"So now you're calling me dumb for stating the obvious?" she seethed, folding her hands tightly over her chest as she gave him a scathing look.

She could see that she'd angered him as the red tint rose to his neck and painted his angry face while his veiny hands clenched and unclenched at his sides.

Andrea took a tentative step back. As if realizing he was starting to scare her, the man released a long weary sigh before turning away. After a minute, he turned back to her and said, "Look, I'll take responsibility for bumping into you. The evidence is there on my headlight, so I'll pay for your paint job, and any other issue you feel may have come from the accident, okay?" he asked passively, indicating he was done with this interaction.

"Don't bother. I can fix my own problems, thank you. I'm not 'dumb' enough to want your help," Andrea quipped, heading for her Jeep.

"I didn't say you were..." the man trailed off, frustrated. "Fine. Do whatever you want, lady," he spat before turning to head for his vehicle.

She watched the man step into his SUV and drive off without a second glance.

"The nerve of that man," Andrea continued to fume after he left her and went on his merry way. She could have been in a major accident because of him, and all he had the nerve to do was blame her for what happened. *Men were so insufferable*, she thought to herself.

After spending a few more minutes calming down and getting back in the right frame of mind, she got back in the car to drive herself home.

"What do you mean it's not a big deal, Andrea? It could have been so much worse. You could have been seriously hurt." Cora's face was marred with sincere concern, the worry lines on her face indicating so.

Andrea had recounted the accident to her sister but

brushed it off as minor so she wouldn't worry her sister. She then looked at Cora with a smile.

"What?" Cora asked.

"Nothing, it just warms my heart, how worried you are about my well-being," she expressed.

"You're my sister, Drea. Of course, I'm going to be worried about you. Especially with the way that Dad died... I'm freaking out with the thought that it almost happened to you too," Cora returned in a chilling voice.

Andrea shivered at the very thought of it. "Yeah, I was so shaken up when it happened. All I could see was how they had detailed Dad's accident and how that was going to happen to me," she confessed.

Cora walked over and engulfed her sister in a tight embrace. Andrea was grateful to have this kind of support. She'd been craving it for so long.

"I'm sorry that happened to you. I'm even happier you're okay."

Andrea relaxed into the hug, loving how natural it felt to be hugged by her sibling.

Cora pulled back and gave her a stern look. "But next time, please be careful. I don't know what I would do if I lost you too."

Chapter Nine

I t was almost a week now since Andrea's return to Oak Harbor. Things had been moving smoothly. She chose a room on the ground floor of the inn to set up her office space. There were still some things that needed to come from her old office, but she delayed it for a bit. Even though Cora had insisted it was pointless to pay for the room, being the inn was theirs, Andrea was adamant.

"This way, the books can be kept up to date, and we don't have to write this off as miscellaneous or such," she expressed. "Besides, I love the feel of being independent."

In the end, Cora had conceded.

She'd also been helping a lot more around the house, helping Cora with the cooking, laundry, and housework. Their mother was determined that she could still manage to do all the things she used to before her diagnosis, but the girls weren't taking any chances.

All in all, the days went by without a hitch.

"Hi, sweetie."

Andrea looked up from wiping down the counter in the

kitchen to see her mother standing by the island in the middle of the room.

"Hi, Mom," she returned, giving her mother a small smile. "How are you feeling?"

Becky hesitated for a moment. Andrea could see the uncertainty in her eyes. She was glad to have her mother back in her life, but at the same time, she knew the relationship they had before she left wasn't as strong as it had once been. Some days it felt as if they were tiptoeing on eggshells around each other.

"I was wondering if you would like to accompany me to the rose garden down on the path," Becky invited.

Andrea thought about it and saw no reason why she shouldn't. Besides, she'd been dying to inspect the garden a bit more.

"Sure, why not." She put down the dishtowel she'd been wiping dishes with and followed her mother out the back door.

She followed her mother along the path, and before she knew it, they were standing before the entrance to the garden. Andrea couldn't help but admire the beauty laid out before her. When her mother pushed open the garden gates, Andrea was in awe as her eyes scanned every which way. She thought the garden was probably only rivaled by the Brooklyn Botanical Gardens— it was that spectacular. There were flowers everywhere, from the rarest and most exotic to the simplest. The place was a haven.

"Your father started sprucing up this area as a birthday and wedding anniversary gift for me on my fiftieth birthday. Ever since, the garden has seen at least one new flower species being added every birthday for the past fifteen years. This year would have made the sixteenth if he hadn't—"

Andrea knew her mother was still mourning her father. She wasn't sure if there would ever be a time that she didn't miss him. She hoped with her and Cora being there that she'd be able to cope with it all.

"I want to show you something. I showed Cora, but I think you need to see it too."

Andrea silently followed her mother further into the garden until they came upon an area with a raised circular platform made from cobblestone with concrete garden benches surrounded by pink and yellow chrysanthemums and peonies.

Just behind the platform and separated from the other flowers was a variety of rosebushes of the most exotic kind she'd ever seen. There were solid and variegated hues and short and long-stemmed bushes.

Andrea rubbed her nose gently against the soft petals of a rose, breathing in the gentle scent.

"This garden was a labor of love from your father," she heard her mother say behind her.

As Becky settled on one of the benches, Andrea took the time to study her. Her mother's once lustrous light brown hair that used to hang all the way down the middle of her back was now just shoulder length and flat, peppered with gray hair. Her once even-toned skin boasted a few wrinkle lines and creases, especially around her eyes. Her mother had transitioned from her once youthful self, and she'd barely gotten the time to notice it until now. Just then, her mother spoke, pulling her out of her reverie.

"I feel like there is something you want to say to me, Drea, but you've been holding back."

Andrea's shoulders slumped as she thought about her mother's statement. One thing about the woman was that she was very perceptive and had always been able to tell whenever one of her children was holding back.

Andrea sighed before walking over to take a seat opposite her mother. "I..." She couldn't formulate what she wanted to say in words.

"I know you blame me as much as you blamed your father for the way he treated you," her mother started.

Andrea looked up at Becky with a pained expression, the hurt surfacing from all those years of wondering why.

"You could have stood up to him. You could have made him see that what he was doing was wrong— to try and force us to take over the business or leave. You just stood there while he went off on me, and you did nothing. Why?" At the end of her strained sentence, tears were streaming down her face as she waited for her mother to say something.

"I am so sorry, Drea. I truly am. I know that to you, it appeared that I did nothing, but I tried to make him see the reason that the inn wasn't your or your sisters' destiny. I tried to make him see that it would cause him to lose you, but in the end, he felt as if he failed as a parent because that's how he had been groomed. As much as he tried to fight it and give you girls all the love in the world, he was conditioned to think that if you didn't want to be a part of the family business, then he had failed as a parent."

Becky reached out and brushed away a few of the tears that still spilled from Andrea's eyes.

"In the end, he couldn't see my logic, and he ended up pushing you away. I tried to help, but you wouldn't take it because you thought it was coming from him, and you girls were just as stubborn as your father."

At that moment, Andrea remembered her mother giving her a wad of cash as she prepared to leave home and to call if she needed anything. She also remembered that she hadn't taken the money but had left it on the bed when she left.

"I wish I had done more, though, and for that, I am sorry, sweetie."

Andrea's heart broke as her mother's tears flowed down her face. "I'm sorry too, Mom," she apologized. "I should have accepted the help you gave, but now I see that I was too proud to accept it and too proud to return home," she confessed as she embraced her mother tightly. The two continued to cry and find solace in each other.

When the crying had subsided, the two pulled apart and smiled at each other. Andrea felt as if a weight had been lifted from her chest, and she was happy her mother had initiated the talk.

"Let me show you something." Her mother rose from the bench and walked back over to the rose bushes, but this time to a rose bush separated from the others.

The blooms were bright orange with pink on their outer circumference. They were extremely beautiful. Andrea wondered how she'd missed them before.

"Your father planted these about six months ago. They were supposed to be my surprise this year. I wasn't aware they were here because he cordoned off the area so that I wouldn't see them. But after his death, I came here and removed the barricade."

Andrea rubbed her mother's arm comfortingly.

Becky turned to her daughter with seriousness in her eyes. "He was planning to surprise me with not just this, but with your presence. He wanted you girls to be here for my next birthday to celebrate with me and to enjoy this." Becky opened her arms, gesturing at the expanse of the garden.

Andrea was floored by the revelation that her father had been taking steps to resolve their issues for some time now. He had wanted to reconcile his family, and deep down, the thought warmed her heart.

When the two made it back to the house, Cora had made it back from the inn. She'd gone to resolve an issue one of their guests was having. Their mother went upstairs to her room to rest.

"So, I saw you and Mom coming from the rose garden," Cora started conversationally. "Did you guys get a chance to talk?"

"We did," Andrea confirmed. "It turns out our family's major problems have stemmed from misunderstandings and pride."

"Hmm."

"You know I was thinking about taking the boat out on the water. Want to come with?" This had been one of the things Andrea was itching to do since her return, and she hoped her sister was game.

"Yes, that sounds like a great idea," Cora readily agreed.

They both headed for their rooms, changing into their swimwear and throwing on sundresses. The two then made their way to the backyard, down by the dock.

Andrea loved the feel of the water spraying against her face as she revved the engine and the boat glided effortlessly through the liquid blue. She liked the fact that she could enjoy doing these things freely that others had to pay for at a resort.

After some time of cruising through the blue-green waters, the sun began to heat up the sky. Andrea brought the boat to a stop on the south side of the Camano Islands, and the two sisters removed their sundresses before making a splash in the clear waters.

Andrea was truly enjoying the coolness of the water as the sun above their heads provided the perfect balancing of temperature.

Half an hour later, the two became tired of swimming and made their way back on the boat. After running fresh water over their skin, they applied the sunscreen they had brought and just lazed on the deck of the boat.

Andrea told Cora about the conversation she'd had with their mother and how much it felt as if a weight had been lifted off her.

"I realize now I can't blame you for what happened to me. You were just a kid yourself, and I was naïve and not at all thinking straight," she confided.

"My life was back on track. But then... I- I..."

She'd explained how she'd been living with her friend Amanda for some months and how she'd gotten a job, but she still couldn't find the words to tell her sister how that job had led to her making the biggest mistake of her life.

"I made so many mistakes, Cora." She sighed, putting her head in her hands.

"Drea, it's okay. You don't have to finish the story now," Cora soothed.

"No," Andrea halted her sister. "I do. I need to get this off my chest."

Her mind flashed back to a day she would never forget, and that always reminded her of how naïve she was. She remembered everything about that day as if it was just yesterday, from the pink sundress she wore and her white sandals to the way her heart beat erratically as she made her way up the driveway of the expansive mansion before her. She remembered being let in to wait by the foyer as the maid went in search of her employer. She remembered giving the maid the slip after being told he wasn't in. She was sure that was a lie which was confirmed the moment she raised her hand and knocked on the door at the far end of the upstairs east wing.

She remembered the look of surprise on his face before it turned to annoyance. She remembered hearing the laughter of a female coming from inside the room as he used his body to expertly block the slight opening in the door. Andrea remembered hitting him as her tears fell. Even though they hadn't been involved for long, she'd thought they were headed somewhere, but just like in the same fashion it started, it ended— like a whirlwind.

She should have known from that night that she wasn't anything special to him— he'd left her the day after their first time together, and she'd awoken to a few bills on the bedside table for her to get a cab home. She'd learned from the housekeeper that he had left to start filming and wouldn't be back anytime soon. For the next two months, she'd called him nonstop without success.

As she stood before him with tears streaming down her face, he had offered no apology but instead had blamed her for being so gullible as to think that he wanted anything from her apart from what they had shared that night. That evening, she left feeling lost and despondent. When she got home, she went straight to the bathroom and released all the content of her stomach before crumbling on the floor and crying herself to sleep.

That day, the stained glass shrouding her vision had fully shattered into a million pieces. Her naivety had caused her to give up the most special thing she had, and there was no way to go back in time to stop herself from making the mistake she'd made. Still, out of it came something so precious, something she could never ever think of parting with.

Chapter Ten

Andrea stretched languidly in bed. She felt refreshed and calm. The past three days had been great. She'd spent more time with her family than she had in over twenty-four years, and she loved it. She'd felt as if a weight had been lifted off her chest after her conversations with Cora and her mother.

Yet, the thought of her daughter's father plagued her occasionally throughout the past seventy-two hours. Cora had encouraged her to tell Rory about her father, but she still wasn't sure that was a good idea. He had only contacted her one time over a month ago, and she doubted he would ever try to do so again. She rationalized that it would do more harm than good to tell her daughter now.

Just then, her phone rang. She swiped the phone from the bedside table and looked at the caller ID to see that it was her daughter.

"Hi, sweetie, I was just thinking about you." She smiled into the phone.

"You were?" She could hear the joy in Rory's voice that triggered her smile to grow even broader.

"I was," she replied. "I was wondering if you had put any more thought into having our wedding here instead of San Francisco."

There was a short pause which caused Andrea to sit up and rest her back against the headboard as she waited for her daughter to speak.

"I don't know, Mom," Rory started hesitantly. "Oak Harbor seems like a great place, but I don't know if it's what I'm looking for," she cautiously stated.

Andrea couldn't help the wave of disappointment that washed over her. She'd been so hopeful that Rory would have eagerly accepted the offer. Nevertheless, the day would be all about her daughter, and she only wanted what was best for her.

"I understand, honey. I'm just asking you to keep an open mind. Maybe if you're able to, you could visit the island, and if you're not totally sold on it, then I won't ever bring it up again," she promised.

"All right, Mom," Rory agreed. "I have some free time coming up in the next month. I'll take you up on it then."

Just like that, Andrea was hopeful once more. "Maybe you could bring my son-in-law with you when you come," she invited. "Speaking of, where is my handsome son-in-law?"

Rory's laughter rang through the receiver. "He's in the living room. Let me go get him for you," she offered.

After a good half a minute of her daughter moving from where she was to get to her fiancé, she heard her speak. "Hey, babe, Mom's on the phone."

"Hi, Mom, how are you?" James's jovial voice rang through. She'd insisted he start calling her Mom after he and Rory had dated for over a year. She preferred not to be called Ms. Hamilton or Ms. Andrea as it made her feel much older than she was.

"Hi, James. How is my favorite son-in-law?" she asked.

James laughed at this. "I am your only son-in-law."

Andrea chuckled. "In my head, I have two more sons-in-law, but you are by far the best one," she countered.

"I won without even trying." James chortled, prompting another giggle from Andrea herself.

"So, how's work?" she asked, changing the subject.

"Work is great, Mom. I should have this case finished by the end of the month," he informed her.

"That's wonderful. I wish you guys weren't so far away. I really miss you both," she confessed.

"Awe, we miss you too, Mom. I know Rory really wishes she could see you more often," he admitted.

"I wish so too. Maybe you guys can move back to Arlington to cut out that three thousand miles we have between us," she suggested, half-jokingly.

It was true. She really did miss her daughter. Sometimes phone calls and FaceTime weren't enough. But Rory was happy, and that was truly what mattered.

"Mom, I'm putting you on speaker. Rory wants to be in the conversation," James informed her.

"Okay, no problem."

"Mom, we'll come to visit you as soon as James's case is over. I promise," she heard her daughter's voice that seemed to be in the distance. "In the meantime, I'll hold off on planning anything for the wedding right now. And who knows, maybe when we visit, we'll fall in love with the place and decide to have everything there. Imagine our wedding in Oak Harbor. Right, James?"

"Oh yeah, right," James replied hastily.

Andrea was sure the venue didn't matter to him. As long as Rory walked down the aisle and said, "*I do*," that would suffice him.

James took the women's discussion of the bridal plans as a way to excuse himself from the conversation to prepare for his client's deposition.

Half an hour later, Rory and Andrea said their goodbyes.

After a few minutes of sitting up in bed and reflecting on the things that had transpired in the week, she finally swung her legs over the edge of the bed, grabbed her toiletries, and walked to the bathroom across the hall from her room.

She allowed the warm water gushing from the showerhead to beat against her back and shoulders, reveling in the heat it generated all throughout her body.

Andrea made her way down the stairs after her shower. She found her mother and sister in the kitchen having breakfast at the island.

"Good morning," she greeted cheerily as she stepped toward the cupboard to get herself a plate.

"Good morning, sweetie. Did you sleep well?" her mother asked.

"I did," Andrea replied, turning to face them once more.

After taking a seat, she scooped a generous serving of the scrambled eggs and bacon sitting in the middle of the island before adding a stack of pancakes on the side.

"I spoke with Rory this morning. She said that she'll think about having her wedding here, but she and her fiancé will have to come here first before they decide."

"Drea, that's wonderful news. I'm sure when they get here, it will be a no-brainer that they have to have it here," Cora said excitedly.

Andrea gave her sister a hopeful smile.

"Before I forget, Tessa called. She's inviting us out for drinks this weekend," Cora told her.

"Okay, I'm game. Sure," she agreed.

She was happy to know that the feeling of togetherness

witnessed at the barbecue hadn't just been an act of politeness but that her cousins sincerely were making an effort to reconnect with them. Last night Kerry and her daughter Nikki had stopped by to drop off a fruit cake and had stayed for dinner. They had spent the time reminiscing over their childhood and regaling Nikki with stories of the adventures they had been on.

"Did she say who else was going?" she asked after some thought.

"Yeah," Cora replied. "She said Sharon, Kerry, Rhonda, and Brian's wife Kirsten will be there."

Andrea couldn't help but wonder if it was such a good idea for her to be in a setting with so many female members of her family. Although she'd opened up to Cora about her time in New York and with Rory's father, she wasn't so sure she would be willing to share that information with the others. These girls' nights usually meant personal questions would be asked that she wasn't ready to answer.

"You don't have to go if you don't want to," she heard her sister say.

Judging by the look of concern on Cora's face, she could determine that Cora was aware that she felt uncomfortable with the situation.

"We can stay in and watch an 'I Love Lucy marathon," Cora offered as an alternative.

"No, that's fine, Sis. I want to," she spoke up. "It'll be great to see and catch up with the whole gang again," she reasoned.

"I'm happy you girls are reconnecting with your cousins. Family is important."

At her mother's statement, Andrea turned to give her a smile. "I'm glad, too, Mom. I thought it would have been more difficult than this, but it's not, and I'm grateful for that," she admitted.

Andrea noticed her mother's eyes were glistening. "Mom," she started to say in concern.

"I just wish Samuel was here to witness this," Becky said softly as a tear ran down her cheek.

Andrea's chest tightened at her mother's vulnerability. She reached over to rest her hand on top of the one her mother had on the table. She didn't have the words to comfort her but instead gave the hand she held a gentle squeeze.

"I know you miss him, Mom. We miss him, too, but somehow I believe he knew that we would find each other again and that we would be here. With everything that he did leading up to his death, he knew," Cora reached over and took her mother's other hand in hers.

"I don't know what I would have done if-if... I'm happy that you girls are here. My sweet angels," their mother expressed through the tears now steadily flowing down her face.

Andrea's gaze remained fixed on her mother's face even as they stung with unshed tears.

Cora got up from her seat and gave her mother a hug from behind, resting her head on her shoulder. "We'll always be here for you, Mom. I promise."

Andrea got up from her seat to envelope both Cora and her mother in her arms as she rested her head on her mother's other shoulder. "We'll always be here for you, Mom," she reaffirmed Cora's earlier statement.

At their declaration, Becky raised her hands to rest her palms against her daughters' cheeks. "I love you both so much... my beautiful girls. What in god's name did I do to have such a wonderful family?" She placed a gentle kiss on each of their foreheads before they released their embrace.

After Becky left to go visit Marg at the inn, Andrea and Cora took the time to work in sync to wash and put away the dishes.

Hearing her sister release a long exhale, Andrea turned to look at her.

"I feel so helpless, knowing this disease is going to rob Mom of her independence sooner than later, and there isn't much we can do about it," Cora expressed as she stood at the sink staring out the window.

"I know," Andrea confirmed. "Sometimes it feels like I'm holding my breath, waiting for her symptoms to get worse. I mean, she's lost so much with Dad dying and her not getting to be a part of our lives and being there for her grandchildren when they were growing up, and now... this sickness wants to rob her, rob us of the time we get to spend together."

Andrea sighed, feeling defeated. She felt her sister's hand on her shoulder, and she turned her head to look at her once more.

"It's going to get a lot harder, but we have to remain strong for her, Drea. I want us to try and get the family more involved so that when the hard times come, we'll always have the memories of these times she got to spend with all of us," Cora encouraged.

Andrea went to answer her sister, but just then, she heard the distinct ringing of her cell phone from upstairs. "Let me go get that."

Cora gestured for her to go ahead.

"I'll be back," Andrea promised before dashing upstairs to retrieve her ringing phone.

She reached for the phone that lay on the bedside table and brought it to her ear.

"Hello?"

"Hello, am I speaking with Andrea Hamilton?" a female's voice inquired from the other line.

"Yes, this is she," Andrea confirmed.

"Please hold for Mr. Pennington."

Shortly afterward, there was a beep before a male's voice came over the line.

"Ms. Hamilton, this is Arthur Pennington, lawyer for Mr. David Latcher and executor of his estate."

At the mention of her daughter's father, her heart slammed against her chest as she waited for the lawyer to continue.

"Ms. Hamilton, it is unfortunate that I have to say this, but Mr. Latcher died three days ago..."

Chapter Eleven

"**A**ndrea, what's wrong?"

Andrea had been standing by the island, staring at nothing in particular for the past few minutes. Nothing seemed to make sense.

"Drea—"

"David Latcher is dead." She barely got through the lump that had taken residence in her throat.

"What?" Cora asked, perplexed. "Who is David Latcher?"

"Aurora's father. He-he-he...he's dead, and he left her something. I don't know what, but his lawyer wants to meet with her, and I don't know what to do," she rushed out in a panic.

"Oh no," was all Cora could say as she recognized the weight of the situation her sister was in. Rushing over to her, she threw her arms around her shoulders and pulled her close.

"Rory's going to hate me, Cora. My god. What have I done..." She broke down as the reality hit her that there was no escape from finally telling her daughter the truth about her father. The pain she felt reverberated from her heart and shook her body with her sobs. "I can't... I can't... tell her this. This is too much..."

"Drea, you'll have to tell her," Cora spoke softly as she ran her hand slowly over the back of her sister's head. "If you don't, you run the risk of the lawyer getting to her, and that will make her feel even more betrayed than if you had told her. At least coming from you, she'll understand why you did it," she continued to reason as Andrea sniffled against her chest.

"I'm scared, Cora. I feel like I'm about to lose my daughter," she managed to get out as her body remained abuzz with the anxiety she felt.

"I know, sweetie, but you just have to be honest with her and soon. If you want me to be there for emotional support when you do, I'll be there," Cora offered.

Andrea pulled away from her sister with an all be it small but grateful smile. "Thanks, Cora."

"Anytime, gummy bear," her sister replied, calling her by one of the endearing nicknames they had for each other. She bumped her shoulder against Andrea's in support.

"I'm going to head down by the inn and finish setting up my office," Andrea informed Cora.

On her walk over to the inn, she chose to take the path behind the house instead of using the walkway on the edge of the driveway that led from the house to the inn. She wanted to use the ten minutes it took to get there to clear her mind.

There were so many times she'd thought about telling Rory the truth about David. The first time was when she'd brought her to meet him to demand he pay child support. She'd been struggling to make ends meet as she tried to juggle her waitressing and bartending work while taking care of her four-year-old and juggling classes at the community college. She was burnt out, and the pay just wasn't taking care of the bills.

"Okay, sweetie, we're going to meet a very special person today," she remembered saying to her daughter as she pulled the

second-hand parka she had bought for her daughter at the Goodwill store on Clinton Ave, Rochester.

"Santa?" her daughter asked excitedly as she moved on to fixing the scarf around her neck before putting on her winter hat.

At her daughter's question, Andrea released a chuckle. "No, sweetie, we're not just there yet. We're still in November, and Santa doesn't come around until December, remember?"

Rory's face fell at her mother's revelation. "Okay," she replied in a small, feeble voice.

"I'll take you to meet Santa next month, I promise," Andrea offered as consolation, not liking when her daughter got disappointed.

"Pinky promise?" The little girl perked up once more at the prospect.

"Pinky promise," she replied, hooking her little finger with her daughter's and shaking it to seal their pact.

"Who are we going to meet then, Mommy?" Rory asked her mother, who was now shrugging on her own coat, to take her daughter out into the chilly environment.

Andrea evaded her daughter's question. "It's a surprise, but a good one, promise."

On the train ride, she'd been nothing but a ball of nerves. She wanted David to acknowledge that he had a daughter and to start helping to take care of her, but at the same time, she was fearful that he would fight for custody and that she would lose her daughter. What she'd not anticipated was him once again throwing her out as if she was nothing but a piece of gum on his shoe but even worse was him calling her child a bastard and telling her never to show her face around him again or he would have her arrested and her daughter placed in foster care.

His refusal to have anything to do with Rory had cut her deep, considering you only had to look at her hair and emerald eyes that resembled his so much to know that it had to be an act of cruel injustice for her not to be his. From that day, David

Latcher had been dead to her, and she committed the ultimate betrayal of her daughter's trust by lying to her about her father.

Still, she'd committed to working ten times harder than she was so that she would be able to give her daughter all she needed, to make her feel loved and never understand the meaning of not being wanted. Within just over a month from her getting that first call to now, it seemed as if everything had been for nothing.

"Hi, sweetie. Is everything all right?" Becky asked her daughter as soon as she stepped into the lobby area of the inn.

Andrea plastered on a smile to appease the worried look her mother was giving her.

"Yes, Mom, I'm good. I just came over here to set up my office. The delivery men should be coming by soon to drop off a few pieces I ordered from Staples in town, and I wanted to be in place for when they get here."

"Okay," her mother replied. "I was just finishing up my daily visit with Marg."

At the mention of the receptionist, Andrea's gaze darted behind her mother to see the raven-haired woman with the large-framed glasses that hid her doe-shaped eyes. Her bright smile could have turned anyone's frown into one that matched her own.

"Hi, Marg. I'm sorry I didn't greet you earlier. I was distracted," she explained as she walked over to the reception-ist's station.

"That's okay, Andrea. I won't fault you for missing me this time," the woman joked.

Her effervescent attitude was so contagious that Andrea couldn't help the giggles that left her lips. She liked Marg. She was drawn in by her personality, so much so that she forgot about her own worries.

"Marg, please just call me, Drea," she implored the woman.

"All of my friends and family do. I can tell that we will become fast friends," she predicted.

"Drea, it is," the woman acquiesced.

Suddenly Andrea had an idea. "Myself, Cora, and some of our cousins are going out this weekend, and it would be great if you could come."

The slight widening of the receptionist's eyes signaled that she was surprised by Andrea's invitation, but she recovered quickly as her grin broadened even more. "Sure, I'd be delighted to go out with you all. I haven't been out in ages."

Andrea looked at her in mock horror. "That is shocking... I can't see it."

At her antics, Marg chortled. "Believe me, I am not that interesting," she said in between her laughter.

Andrea gave her a long, weird look. "I still can't see it," she replied.

Marg gave her a wry smile. "I just haven't had a reason to go out in a while," she replied simply.

Andrea imagined there was more to that statement but chose not to push in case she made her uncomfortable.

"Well, you're invited and don't even think about getting out of it. I'll find your home and dress you if I have to," she warned. "Everyone deserves some time out from this tedious drab thing we call life."

At her statement, Marg gave her a grateful smile. "I'll come. I promise, and I never go back on my promises."

"Good," Andrea responded, pleased by the woman's response. "I'm going to go set up my equipment until the truck gets here," she informed her mother.

"Okay, honey. Do you need any help?" her mother offered.

"No, that's fine, Mom. Finish your talk with Marg."

Andrea spent the next hour fixing up the room she'd rented on the ground floor of the inn. It was one of the only three enclosed spaces on that floor— it and the kitchenette and dining area where the guests could utilize the state-of-the-art appliances for cooking if they didn't wish to utilize the services of the restaurant. There was also a staff bathroom used mainly by Marg and some maid staff that cleaned the rooms. The rest of the downstairs featured the large foyer with a section designed for the receptionist's station, a grand double staircase, and further to the back, a sitting area decked with plush sofas and armchairs and a brilliant view of the outside through the French windows and door lining the entire south wall. From there, she could also see the newly constructed gazebo, and she had to admit it was a work of art.

After she'd set up her equipment, the movers came and dropped off two comfortable gray armchairs, a heavy-duty desk and chair, a folding table, and a bright orange ottoman. It wasn't as vibrant as her old office, but it would suffice.

For the next four hours after setting up her office, Andrea spent the time holed up there working, answering emails, turning down offers to add more clients and referring them to her colleagues who she knew would be a good fit, and simply keeping her mind off the current problem at hand.

Cora had visited her in the past hour, and Marg had ordered lunch from the restaurant for her. She hadn't realized how famished she'd been until the savory scent of the food triggered her stomach that let out an embarrassing rumble.

It wasn't until close to the evening that Andrea decided she'd done enough for the day. When she made it back to the house, instead of relaxing, she changed into her running gear.

"I'm going for a run," she informed Cora, who was in the kitchen preparing dinner.

"Okay," her sister replied. "Next time, we can go together."

"Yeah, that'd be great," Andrea agreed.

As the time ticked away, Andrea's chest felt as if it was on fire from how hard she was running. The muscles in her legs began to tighten, and she knew it was an indication that she needed to stop. Still, she pushed herself. Just as she made the turn at the intersection of Maui unto Torpedo Road, she hit a hard wall that sent her crashing backward with her arms flailing.

"Eek!" Andrea instinctively tried to twist her body sideways as her arm extended from her side, but with force. Going down, she doubted she would come out unscathed.

However, before her body could make an impact with the asphalt, she felt strong hands wrap around her arms and quickly pull her upward once again.

"It seems you have a knack for getting yourself into accidents," she heard the raspy voice above her head say.

Realizing that whoever it was that had just saved her from injury was still holding her, she began to step away from the gentleman, and his hands fell away from her. When she finally raised her eyes to see who it was, they widened to the size of saucers at who stood before her.

"You!"

Chapter Twelve

"**Y**ou!" she echoed.

Andrea couldn't believe that the man standing before her was the same one that had hit her car just a few days ago. What were the odds that they would be involved in two collisions in less than a week? Oak Harbor wasn't a big town, but it wasn't that small either that you would just randomly run into a stranger you've never met before twice in one week.

"Me," the gentleman replied, breaking into her musings.

She found herself assessing the man before her. His dark blond hair was cut low at the sides while the hair on top of his head was longer, a few strands falling into his eyes. His deep-set sapphire blue eyes sat high on his angular face, and he had laugh lines at the corner of each eye and his mouth. She guessed he was probably in his mid-forties or older. He was at least six inches taller than her five-foot-four height.

"Are you all right?"

She jumped, surprised by the hand waving before her face. "Yes, sorry. What were you saying?"

The man gave her a weird look before he replied, "I was saying if we keep meeting like this, pretty soon one of us is bound to end up in the hospital." When she didn't immediately make a comment, he continued, "I'm sorry we got off on the wrong foot earlier—"

"No, I'm sorry. I shouldn't have stopped so suddenly. I just wasn't aware someone was behind me, and I didn't see the light until it was too late. It's my fault. I take full responsibility for the accident."

By the look of his surprise, Andrea was certain he had not expected the apology.

Catching himself gaping, he fixed his expression before responding. "It's okay. It could have happened to any of us. I'm sorry I lost my temper with you. I'm not usually like that, but I just had a lot on my mind, and I took it out on you. It really doesn't excuse my behavior."

"It's not entirely your fault," she interrupted. "I think I pushed a little too hard back there; you were bound to snap." She grinned sheepishly.

The man chuckled, and the sound seemed to shake his whole body. "You were pretty spot on with your words. I won't lie."

Andrea shrugged in apology as a small smile graced her lips.

"Let's see if we can leave on a better footing this time, so the next time we meet, we won't be going for the jugular," he offered.

She stared at him in confusion until he held out his hand to her.

"Donny Hasgrove. It's a pleasure to meet you, Mrs.?"

"It's just Miss. I'm Andrea Hamilton," she replied, placing her hand in his outstretched one.

"It is a pleasure to officially meet you, Miss Andrea Hamilton." He beamed, showing off even, white teeth.

The hand that held hers, she noticed, was calloused and firm. She suspected that he was used to hard work. "It's a pleasure to meet you, too, Mr. Hasgrove. Again, I'm sorry about the accident. If you'd like, I can pay for any damage that might have been done to your car."

The man shook his head in refusal. "That won't be necessary. I already got it covered. I'm just happy we were able to clear up our misunderstanding."

"Well, I guess I'll see you around then."

He gave her another smile before heading in the opposite direction. She was happy she'd gotten the chance to clear up the misunderstanding, and the more she thought about it, Donny Hasgrove seemed like an okay person.

When she made it back to the house, she headed for the stairs and went up to her room. She needed to take a shower as she'd felt the sweat running from her scalp down her neck from how hard she'd been pushing herself.

After taking a hot shower, there was a knock at her door as she sat on her bed, running the towel through her wet hair. She looked up just in time to see her sister step through the door.

"Hey, how was your run?" Cora greeted her.

"It was good," she replied. "I actually ran into the gentleman that I met in the accident with... like literally ran smack into him." Andrea brought her hands together, making a smacking sound for effect.

Cora stepped further into the room until she was leaning against Andrea's old study desk. "How did that go?" she asked, now interested in the story.

"Well, he caught me before I collided with the pavement and ripped half my skin off," she replied with a light chuckle.

Cora gave her sister a deadpan look. "And?"

"And... I apologized for not paying attention. For stopping so suddenly before him, and then he apologized for losing his temper," she rushed out. She averted her eyes out of guilt, remembering that she hadn't told her sister the full story of how the man had ended up ramming her Jeep.

Cora's expression was contemplative before transforming to one of incredulity when she finally caught on. "Wait, what? Are you telling me that the accident wasn't actually that man's fault?"

"Well..." Andrea started off, keeping her eyes directed away from her sister's face, "Technically, he ran into my back, so..."

"Drea, this is serious. Why were you so distracted?"

"I was thinking about how much I missed having my family and friends around me for the past twenty-four years. I don't know... I guess I was just feeling guilty that I sort of cut ties with everyone, and then Dad died, and I couldn't tell him how much I missed him." Her voice broke, and she found it hard to continue.

She felt the bed dip before her sister's arm came over her shoulder and pulled her into her embrace.

"I know it's hard knowing that Dad is gone and that we didn't get the chance to reconcile, but trust me. I've had some moments of sadness that felt as if I would break, but we're here now, and we've got each other to get through this. We're making new memories," Cora encouraged her.

Andrea rested her head on her sister's shoulder, happy for the comfort it provided just to have her this close.

"Thanks, Cora," she said after some time of them sitting in the same position.

"Anytime, gummy bear."

After Cora left, Andrea spent the next ten minutes drying her hair before putting it up in a messy bun. She then made her way downstairs to join her family for dinner.

"Before I forget, Captain Braun, one of your father's old colleagues, called. He wanted to speak with you."

Andrea looked up from scooping food onto her fork to see

that her mother was looking directly at her from across the table.

"Me?" she asked, surprised. "What for?"

"He said something about making a page, or is it a website," her mother replied, head inclined and a hand on her chest as she tried to remember the man's exact words.

"I'm not sure I'm the person he's looking for then, Mom. I do social media and Facebook Ads, not website building," she explained to her mother.

"Why don't you give him a call? He left his number, and I think I might have jumbled the message," her mother implored her.

"Okay, I'll call him after dinner," she agreed.

Andrea and Cora cleaned up after the meal while their mother retired to her room. Cora left to call her daughters, and Andrea decided to call the captain to see what he needed.

"Hi, Captain Braun. This is Andrea Hamilton. You asked for me earlier?"

"Yes. Thank you for calling back. I know this might have been sudden and all, but I'm glad you're choosing to take on this project—"

"Oh no, I didn't..."

"Your father spoke so highly of you. He explained you were an expert at what you did, so when I heard you were in town, I knew I just had to ask you to do this for us."

Andrea was surprised by his statement. Her father had been keeping up with her career. He knew enough to be boasting to his friends about her. This knowledge warmed her heart as a slight smile graced her lips. In that instant, she decided to do the project if only to honor the memory of her father, who thought so highly of her even if he didn't get the chance to say it to her face.

"I'd be delighted to be a part of your project, Captain

Braun. Just for clarity, what exactly is it that you need me to do?"

The captain explained to her that he needed her to revamp the fire department's website to make it more user-friendly and informative about the programs and initiatives they have available.

"I'll be sending my lieutenant over. He should get there in the next fifteen minutes. Any information you need, he'll be able to give it to you. I hope that's okay with you."

"Thank you, Captain Braun. That's completely fine. I'll keep an eye out for him."

After hanging up, Andrea decided to take her laptop out to the front porch to finish up some work while she waited for the lieutenant to arrive.

Fifteen minutes later, Andrea could see the headlights of a vehicle coming up the path. Placing the laptop down, she went to stand by the porch column as she watched the dark-colored SUV pull up to the driveway and come to a stop near the designated visitor's parking area. She was surprised at who stepped out of the vehicle.

Even though darkness had fallen, the parkway lights were bright enough for her to make him out clearly. This evening, he wore a navy blue short-sleeved shirt with epaulets on the shoulders, crests on the sleeves, and one above his heart. This was tucked into his navy-blue slacks. His blond hair sported a partial side part, and the strands were slicked down neatly. As he walked toward the porch briskly, his eyes remained trained on the black wristwatch he wore.

Sensing her eyes on him, the man looked up. As recognition flashed in his eyes, he froze in his tracks.

"If I didn't know any better, I would have to think you were the one stalking me, Mr. Hasgrove," she joked, taking the next few steps off the porch to meet him.

The man chuckled. "This is quite the surprise, Ms. Hamilton," he spoke as he shook the hand she held out to him. "I wasn't aware you were Samuel Hamilton's daughter," he continued to say.

Andrea gave him a weak smile. "Well, now you know."

"I must express my own condolences to you. Mr. Hamilton was a good man. Someone I truly respected."

She gave him another rueful smile. "It turns out everyone else knew the type of man my father was better than I did."

Donny's brows drawing together made her realize that she'd said that out loud.

"Shall we get to it?" she asked cheerily, hoping he would forget her earlier statement.

"Huh? Yeah, sure."

He followed her onto the porch, where she offered him a seat in one of the plush armchairs as she sat in another facing him.

She got straight into it. "To tell you the honest truth, I don't create websites for my clients. I do Facebook advertising, but seeing as I'm back in Oak Harbor and I have a little time on my hands, I decided to provide my services."

"Okay, thanks, I guess," Donny replied, unsure. After taking in a long breath and releasing it slowly, he fixed his sharp blue eyes on her. "I'm not really into technology like that, but whatever you need, I'll make sure you have it. Captain says this project is important to the improvement of the department, so I am all for it," he informed her.

"I'm happy to hear that. I take it that you're very dedicated to your job," she observed.

"It's been my life for over twenty years, ten back in Chicago and ten here. The people I work with are my family, and so whatever I can do to shed a positive light on our department, I'm your man."

Andrea smiled at this, realizing that this was a man after her own heart. Like her, he was dedicated to his work, and he loved what he did. She could see that this project wouldn't be so bad after all.

After setting an appointment to come by the fire station to interview the firefighters and take some pictures of them and the station for the website, Donny left for work, and Andrea used the time to update her Google Calendar before retiring to bed.

Chapter Thirteen

Andrea opened her eyes to total darkness. Looking over at the digital clock on the bedside table, she realized it was four in the morning. It was still early, but it was Saturday, the first weekend since her return to Oak Harbor.

She remained in bed, enjoying the stillness of the morning. She usually savored these early hours on the weekends as it was her time to go through all that had happened throughout the week, those things that went well, those that went bad, and those that she had no control over. She used these times to reset and recalibrate.

Since coming back to Oak Harbor, she'd reconnected with her uncle and aunts and her cousins. She'd learned that her friend Shelby was married to one of her schoolmates she least expected to return to Oak Harbor. She'd forgiven her mother for her perceived abandonment. Cora had become her tower of strength and her sounding board. Rory's father died and, in death, was threatening their relationship, and she had two accidents with the same gentleman with who she would have to be working closely to create a website for the fire department. It was funny how the universe made everything come full circle sometimes.

She spent half an hour going over it all, and when it became evident that she could not go back to sleep, she decided to head downstairs. Going into the refrigerator, she took out the ingredients needed to make her mother's special homemade cinnamon rolls. She figured her family would be up by the time the cinnamon rolls were done.

After combining the ingredients and ensuring the dough was soft and slightly sticky, she dusted the counter with flour before putting it down and using the rolling pin to flatten it. She then spread the cinnamon-flavored filling over the dough before rolling it and cutting it up. After placing them on the baking tray, she coated them with heavy cream and then placed them into the preheated oven to bake for the next half hour.

She then prepared boiled eggs, waffles, bacon, Italian sausage, and freshly squeezed orange juice.

"Mmm... it smells like heaven in here," Cora said as soon as she stepped through the entryway.

"I thought it would be nice to cook for a change," Andrea threw over her shoulder.

"I'm not complaining, and judging by how my stomach has been rumbling since I came in here, it's not complaining either. Well, other than wanting to eat now, but you understand," Cora remarked, then let out a little yawn.

Andrea laughed at her sister's rambling. "Everything will be ready in five minutes, tops. I'm just waiting for the rolls to finish, then we can eat."

"How long have you been down here?" Cora asked.

"Close to three hours," she confessed.

"Good morning, my beautiful daughters," Becky greeted as she waltzed into the room, cutting off whatever Cora had been prepared to say.

"Good morning, Mom. Are you hungry?"

"Well, if I wasn't, I don't think I would be able to resist a bite of all this." Becky gestured to the presentation before her.

"I made your cinnamon rolls recipe too," Andrea revealed just as the oven timer went off.

"You girls are spoiling me too much," their mother spoke with so much feeling.

"You deserve it, Mom. We're making up for lost times," Cora replied while pulling out a stool for her mother to sit by the island.

As soon as the food was scooped onto their plates and they had recited grace, the women dug into the delicious food before them.

"So, where are you girls heading this evening?" Andrea heard her mother ask.

Cora was the one to answer her questions.

"We're going to The Anchor," Cora informed Becky.

"Oh, that's a lovely place. I'm sure you'll all enjoy yourselves. Have fun but be safe."

Both Andrea and Cora acknowledged their mother's warning. They knew it came from a place of motherly care but also that it was linked to the anxiety she had after losing her husband. After Becky finished her breakfast, she left to go visit Marg at the inn while the two sisters fell into their routine of washing and drying the dishes.

"I was thinking that we should renovate the inn," Andrea suggested.

At her statement, Cora looked over at her. "Renovate how?"

"Nothing major, maybe just switch out the furniture in the lobby area for some more modern pieces and probably a few art pieces. But what I really think we should do is repaint it. All of it." Andrea looked from the corner of her eye, waiting for her sister to comment.

Cora stopped drying the dish in her hand as she contemplated Andrea's suggestions. "That's not such a bad idea," she finally agreed. "When you said repaint, though, did you mean the outside of the inn?"

"And inside too. I looked in a few of the unoccupied guestrooms, and I thought they looked dull. I mean, they've been sporting the same wallpaper from when we were kids, and while I'm not too fond of the old furniture either, I'm thinking of tearing off that drab wallpaper and applying a fresh coat of paint. It could really do wonders," she returned.

"But the wallpaper is part of the appeal of making the rooms look authentically vintage," Cora reasoned.

"I understand your sentimental attachment, Cora, but if I were a guest, I wouldn't be all that enthused about staying in a room with peeling wallpaper no matter how much I am a lover of the rustic lifestyle."

Cora contemplated her sister's words before shrugging in acceptance. "Okay. If you think it will boost the appeal to our guests, then let's do it."

Andrea smiled at her triumph.

"Maybe discuss it with Marg. She's been here for a long time, so I think her input could be helpful."

"Yes, sure thing," Andrea agreed.

Cora gave her a curt nod. "Let me know what will be needed so that I can update our books."

Andrea nodded in agreement as they resumed washing and drying the dishes. When they were finished, they made their way out of the kitchen to start on their individual tasks.

Cora paused on the stairs and turned to her sister, who was making her way toward the front door. "Oh, I forgot. I saw a car leaving our driveway last night. Do you have any clue who it was?"

"Yeah. That was Donny Hasgrove. He's the lieutenant at the Oak Harbor Fire Station. I'll be working closely with him to get their website up and running. He's also the man that I had the accident with."

"What?" Cora asked, stumped by her sister's revelation. "That's bizarre."

"I know," Andrea agreed with a chuckle. Taking out her phone and scrolling through her contacts, she beckoned for her sister to come closer. "He has a photo up at his contact. Take a look," she invited, holding up the phone to her face.

Cora took the phone from her sister's hand to stare at the photo. "That's a handsome man," she complimented. "I can see why you chose to do the project," she continued, fixing Andrea with a knowing glance.

"What? No," Andrea quickly refuted. "I'm not interested in Donny. I took the project because I have some time on my hands."

The look on Cora's face told Andrea that her sister was not convinced by her explanation.

"So, you're telling me you didn't notice how handsome he is?" Cora asked in disbelief.

Andrea released her breath slowly. "I'm not saying that, Cora... I'm just not interested in a relationship right now."

Cora folded her arms over her chest as she stared pointedly at her sister. "When have you ever tried to make time for the possibility of a relationship, Drea?"

Andrea sighed again before pursing her lips.

"You can't let what that man did to you rob you of finding someone who will treat you the way you truly deserve. I'm not just saying this because you're my sister, but you have so much to offer, and any man would be lucky to have you "

"Cora..." Andrea turned her back to her sister, annoyed at her for using the knowledge that she hadn't been in a relationship in so long to deflate her reason.

"I remember when we were younger, you had so many dreams and aspirations. One of them was marrying your prince charming and having a family. It's still possible, Drea. I know a lot has happened, an—"

"Life happened, Cora," she interrupted her sister. "I can't... I won't..." Andrea blew the air out through her mouth. "I don't want to talk about this now. I need to go see Marg. I'll see you in a few."

With that, Andrea turned toward the door once more. She didn't see the pained expression that crossed her sister's face as she exited the house.

"Hi, Andrea, you just missed your mom. She left through the back. She said she wanted to go visit her rose garden."

"Oh no, I wasn't looking for Mom. I'm actually here to speak with you," Andrea informed the woman who still wore her uniform, which was a baby blue tunic top with the words *Willberry Inn* stitched over the right pocket and black slacks.

Andrea made a note to speak with Cora to possibly have the staff working during the weekends wearing casual attire.

"Okay," Marg responded, surprised. "Is it about going out later? I promise you I'm coming," she continued to say.

Andrea couldn't help the smile that came to her lips as she listened to Marg trying to guess why she was by the inn.

"I trust you, Marg. I don't believe you would go back on your words intentionally," she assured the woman. "I actually wanted to speak with you about repainting the inn," she informed her.

"All of it?"

"Yes," she confirmed, laughing at the way Marg's eyes lit up with hope behind her glasses. "I spoke with Cora, and she agreed that this place needs a fresh coat of paint to spruce up its appeal. You know this place so well. I want to know what are your thoughts and suggestions. I want you to work closely with me on this."

"Wow, I'm honored. Whatever you need. I'm your person; day or night, I'll be there," Marg offered.

Andrea marveled at the woman's enthusiasm. She could tell that she really loved the inn just from how she interacted with the guests currently staying at the property. On two separate occasions, she'd witnessed Marg offering to call the restaurant to make special meal requests and retelling the history of Willberry Inn, all with a bright smile. She never heard her complain or saw a frown on her face.

"I think it would be great if we went with some bright colors to add vibrancy to the rooms and placed a few more abstract art pieces in the hallways and..." Marg gave Andrea an apologetic smile. "I'm sorry. I get carried away when it comes to renovations and designing. It's a pet peeve of mine."

"That's fine. I'm actually grateful that you aren't afraid to share this," Andrea assured her. "Marg, you're a woman after my own heart. I love your dedication and the way it seems you go all out. Your husband and children must worship the ground you walk on."

The wide smile that brightened her face suddenly fell as something flashed through her eyes. *Is that pain?*

"Marg—"

Marg repositioned her glasses before giving Andrea a quick glance. "Could you excuse me for a minute? I need to use the restroom."

Andrea watched helplessly as the petite woman darted from behind her desk and headed for the bathroom, head bowed.

Ten minutes later, Marg returned to her station, where Andrea stood still, confused by her reaction. Andrea noted that she'd washed her face possibly to hide the evidence of her tears, but her eyes, though behind the barrier of her glasses, shone through a bright red.

"Marg, if I said something out of line, I'm so sorry. I didn't mean to be insensitive. I—"

"It isn't what you said, Andrea. You just caught me off

guard, but that's a story for another time, and I'm fine. I promise," the woman assured her.

Andrea wasn't so convinced. She was certain her words
had triggered possibly a bad memory for the woman, perhaps a
deceased husband or child. She decided to leave it for now. She
would have to get the information from her mother so that she
knew how to approach conversations with her going forward.

The two women spent the next fifteen minutes going over
paint color options and debating whether or not wallpaper
should be used in the kitchen and bathrooms.

"I think it's time to head off home. I'll see you tonight,
Marg."

Andrea turned on her heel and started walking back to the
house. She still felt bad that she'd upset Marg but knew it
would be good for all of them to get out and share some girl
time together.

That was something she most definitely needed.

Chapter Fourteen

"**Y**ou did not do that."

"I have the scar to prove I did."

Andrea laughed at the two women bickering back and forth in the booth they had reserved for their get-together at The Anchor.

"Kerry, if you went, I would have known," Tessa, Kerry's older sister, resolved.

Without warning, Kerry raised herself up while lifting her blouse to her midriff before pointing to a small, barely notice-able mark at the side of her ribcage.

The other women who sat at the booth leaned forward to get a closer look at the mark.

"That is ink," Kirsten, Brian's wife, confirmed. The other women shook their heads in agreement while Tessa's mouth remained agape out of sheer disbelief.

"Oh my God, you did it," she finally managed to say, still looking at her sister with a shocked expression.

"I did, but it's more like a large beauty mark. As soon as the needle touched my skin, I couldn't manage the pain, and I hightailed it out of there." Kerry shivered as if still remembering the pain of the needle.

"But you were only fifteen."

Kerry gave her sister an apologetic look. "There're a lot of things I did that I'm not proud of," she replied simply, bringing the glass of beer to her lips.

Andrea brought her own glass to her lips as she thought about all the reckless things she herself did after leaving Oak Harbor. She could definitely concur with her cousin's statement.

"We've all done things we're not proud of or too keen to talk about." Andrea turned her head to her cousin's wife, who had spoken. Sharon looked wistfully into her own glass of beer.

"Some things you wish you could do over, but then you realize if you actually did get the chance to do it over, you probably wouldn't; not with how much would be at stake." Andrea was surprised that those words had left her lips, but then Kerry responded.

"I know what you mean. For example, take my marriage to Darren. I knew it was a mistake to marry him just because I had Tracy, but I did it anyway because I wanted my child to have a normal childhood. But then Emma came, and I felt trapped because I couldn't get to pursue my passion. There were happy times, don't get me wrong, but when the passion died, and the children were almost grown, we realized that we weren't even friends— just two people coexisting under the same roof for the sake of our kids."

Kerry sighed with her hand on her cheek. "There are so many things I wish I could change, but then if I was able to, I couldn't because that would mean giving up on the opportunity of being a mother to my two wonderful girls, and I can't envision a life without them in it."

The women around the table nodded in understanding, and Andrea caught Cora's own look of understanding.

Just then, their bartender came by to refill their mugs with beer. Cora got a root beer because she'd driven herself and Andrea to the establishment. The others had come by Uber. Andrea raised the frothy brown liquid to her lips before taking a sip and placing it back on the table.

Fixing her eyes on her cousin, Brian's wife, she asked, "So, Kirsten, you're a teacher?" She was deliberate in trying to get the rather quiet woman to participate in the conversation rather than the one-line sentences she'd been offering up in the one hour they'd been at the bar. She figured the woman was probably shy around her, Cora, and their friends because she wasn't used to them, but she was also hoping that the more she got involved in the conversation, the more comfortable she'd get being around them. From the smiles of approval that flitted across Tessa's and Kerry's faces, she could tell they were happy about her efforts.

"Oh yeah... Yes, I teach at Oak Harbor Elementary, fourth grade," she responded softly.

"She taught my son, Ricky."

Andrea raised her brows in surprise at Shelby. "Really? I didn't know you knew Kirsten."

Shelby gave a slight shrug as she replied. "Not really. Ricky was in Kirsten's class five years ago. Randy attended most of the PTA meetings for Ricky. I was responsible for Angela and Isaac," she explained.

"Now I remember. Richard Barrett," Kirsten spoke as it dawned on her that she knew Shelby or was at least acquainted with her.

The conversation continued to flow, as did the drinks, and within the second hour, everyone had loosened up and were laughing and sharing stories.

Andrea looked over at Marg to see that she, too, sported a huge smile on her lips and was getting along well with her family and friends. She was happy she'd chosen to come to the event and had invited her and Shelby.

* * *

"What do you think about this color?"

"Hmm...I don't hate it, but I don't particularly like it," Andrea replied with a shrug.

"Okay... what about this one?" Marg asked, pointing to another wallpaper pattern in the home décor book they were perusing.

"Yes. This looks more like it," Andrea approved.

Two days had already passed since they'd all gone out to The Anchor. The two had been working since the crack of dawn, removing the old faded wallpaper in the downstairs kitchen of the inn. It had been far more work than Andrea had anticipated. They had to cover all exposed areas in the room (except the walls) with plastic and tarpaulin, cut the lights and cover the electrical outlets with tape. They had to soak the walls with warm water and wallpaper stripper before using the putty knives to start stripping off the paper. Afterward, they had to clean the walls with soap and water. All this work lasted all the way into the afternoon.

It had been a grueling experience, but she enjoyed it, especially with Marg's company.

"I don't think I thanked you for inviting me out with your family last evening. I wanted to tell you I had a really great time."

Andrea smiled, acknowledging the woman's sincerity. "It was no big deal, Marg. I'm just happy you came. As long as you're available, you'll always be welcome to join our get-togethers," she promised.

Marg, in turn, gave her a smile of gratitude.

"I'm going to head back to the house, but hopefully, we can pick this up tomorrow."

"Sure, no problem."

After saying her goodbyes, Andrea left.

When she stepped into the house, she noted that it was quiet as she made her way to the kitchen. She realized that it was empty along with the other rooms downstairs. She wondered if Cora may have perhaps gone on the road, but then she recalled that her vehicle was still in its parking spot. Her uncle's black Grand Cherokee was also in the parking lot. This made it even stranger that she couldn't hear or see anyone. Perhaps they were outside.

Pushing open the back door, she walked out onto the porch before taking the two steps that led to the short pavement and to the patio. She still didn't see any sign of her family. Just as she turned to go back inside, her eyes caught two people sitting at the picnic table at the side of the house overlooking the harbor. She changed directions and walked over to the picnic table.

"Hey, Cora, Uncle Luke," she called out as soon as she was in hearing range.

They both turned toward her, and her heart slammed against her chest at the grim expressions on their faces.

"What's wrong?" she asked as soon as she was standing before them. "Is it Mom? Is she okay?" she couldn't help the panic that had crept into her voice as she envisioned the worse scenario.

"Mom's fine, Drea...for now," Cora replied with a deep sigh.

"What does that mean?" she asked, still on alert.

"I didn't tell you this, but the week after the funeral, after you guys left, we took Mom to dinner at the restaurant... and her hand froze, making the fork fall from her grip." Cora looked up at her sister with a pained expression. "She couldn't use that hand for the rest of the meal, Drea," she finished softly. "She was really embarrassed."

Andrea's heart fell to the pit of her stomach.

"The doctor said she suffered a mild case of spasticity and that it will become more prevalent and debilitating the further she regresses. There is a new trial opening up that could possibly give her a few more years, but she is refusing to do it," Cora finished with a defeated sigh.

Andrea's eyes widened in surprise. "Bu-but why?" she stuttered out.

"Mom says she doesn't want to spend the remainder of her life in observation rooms going from trial to trial. She says she wants to spend the time with her family." Cora bowed her head and folded her hands over her chest.

"Cora, she's making a mistake. We have to convince her otherwise."

Just then, Uncle Luke chimed in. "Girls, I know it is a lot to take in, but you can't force your mother to do what she doesn't want to do. If you do that, you will end up regretting it...What Becky needs right now is to know that you're here for her. I know it's not easy, believe me, I know, but just letting her see you supporting her in this difficult time will make the difference that is most needed."

Andrea noted the look of sadness reflected in her uncle's eyes and could only determine that it was as a result of him losing a brother, having a sister who was almost immobile, and a sister-in-law that was more like a sister with ALS. These things could take a toll on a person.

"You're right, Uncle. I'll do my best to support Mom's wishes," she acquiesced, resting a hand on his shoulder to offer some level of comfort to him as well.

"Me too," Cora chimed in, taking his hand into hers and giving it a hearty squeeze. "This may not be what I want, but

I'll support her and make the best of the time we have." Cora offered a small smile that the others returned.

"Thanks for being here for her and for us, Uncle. We couldn't have done it without you."

Uncle Luke squeezed Andrea's hand in acknowledgment. "That's what family is for."

The trio sat by the table, looking out at the water, allowing the peace and tranquility to quiet their tormented minds. Half an hour later, Andrea and Cora went inside, and Uncle Luke left to go pick up his wife Maria from the local library.

After grabbing a bite to eat, Andrea left Cora in the kitchen and headed up to her room. She needed to take a shower after the long day she'd had.

After her shower, she pulled her laptop out of the desk drawer to go through and answer her emails. As much as her cell could perform all those functions, she didn't utilize it for that. She preferred answering her emails the way she'd always done it.

One particular email caught her attention, and she quickly pulled it up.

"Good day, Miss Hamilton,

Regarding our conversation last week, I would like to officially welcome you to Oak Harbor Fire Department. We are happy to have you join our family for however long you will be with us.

You are welcome to stop by at any time that is convenient and a representative will always be on hand to answer your questions, provide information on the department's operations and make your time with us as smooth as possible.

Thank you again for your willingness to engage with us and I look forward to working with you.

Best Regards,

Donny Hasgrove

Lieutenant

Oak Harbor Fire Department"

After shooting Donny an email thanking him for his warm welcome, she went to the closet to change her clothes before grabbing her camera case and heading out.

"I'm heading out to the fire station. I'll be back in a few," she informed Cora, who sat on the porch admiring the view.

"Okay, be safe."

"Thanks, Sis. I will."

Chapter Fifteen

T he moment Andrea pulled up to the fire station, she knew that she would be enjoying this project a whole lot. It would be a change from her regular and profitable Facebook Ad consultancy job, but she wasn't worried. This was far easier than what she normally did, a little bit more time-consuming and hands-on, but nevertheless easier.

Taking out her camera, she took a few photos of the entrance and the hangar-like structure at the front that currently held two fire trucks and an ambulance. As she stepped through the entrance, she realized there was no one around, but there were a set of stairs at the back, and she could hear noise coming from above. She could also see that there were a set of rooms on the landing along a long corridor that overlooked the truck hangar. After snapping a few more photos of the protective gears neatly stacked on shelves attached to the walls, she made her way up the stairs leading to the first floor.

The first room she passed along the corridor was a kitchenette, and the next two rooms looked like offices. When she made it to the final room, which was much larger than the others, she could see through the window that there were a number of lounge chairs and couches scattered throughout. A number of men in the same tunic she'd seen Donny in were relaxing on the furniture. She turned off the flash of her camera so she wouldn't startle them and to get a few candid photos. Andrea aimed the device and snapped in quick succession. As she moved further around toward the door, she saw Donny slightly turned away from her, laughing with one of his colleagues. Andrea smiled at his notable ease. She raised the camera and snapped him. As if sensing her presence, he looked over his shoulder and caught her eye through the glass. Andrea gave him a simple wave. Donny turned to say something to the man, who in turn looked in her direction before he turned and came toward the door.

"Miss Hamilton, I wasn't aware you would be coming here today. I could have better prepared the—"

"Oh no, that's fine. I'm actually happy you didn't know I was on my way here. It gave me a better chance at catching you in your element, not just what you think is to be presented. And please just call me Andrea," she greeted him back.

"Okay," he agreed. "You seem to have a knack for catching me off guard." He laughed as he ushered her into the room. "Please come in. Let me introduce you to the rest of the guys."

As soon as she entered the room, her anxiety reared up as the men stared at her, not saying anything.

"Guys, this is Andrea Hamilton. She's the one who will be restructuring our website."

"Hello everyone, it's a pleasure to meet you all," she greeted with a smile.

"It's a pleasure to meet you, too, Miss Hamilton," one of the men broke the awkward silence that had settled over the room to greet her.

"You didn't tell us she would be this pretty lieutenant," another called out.

Andrea felt her cheeks warming over and was certain her cheeks were bright red.

"Nice to meet you, Miss Hamilton. It's always a pleasure to have another female around every once in a while."

Andrea caught herself before the gasp left her lips. She gave the woman who was currently sporting a low buzz cut and looked to be about four inches taller than her a smile.

"Please call me, Andrea," she implored as she shook the woman's hand.

Soon enough, the others lined up to shake her hand and welcomed her to their fire station. Everyone resumed their previous positions and conversations, and for that, she was grateful.

"So, how long have you worked here?" she asked the only female in the fold whose name she found out was Celeste.

"Five years," she answered.

Andrea shook her head, contemplating.

"I know what you really want to ask."

"Really?" Andrea questioned the woman's bold statement.

"Yup. I bet you want to know why I chose to become a fire-fighter."

Andrea laughed. "That may have been one of the questions on my list," she confessed.

The woman chuckled.

"So, why did you?"

Celeste placed her hand over her chest as she stared ahead. Andrea wondered if she was going to answer the question, considering how long she took to open her mouth.

"My house burned down when I was eight because the response of the fire team was too slow. We all managed to get out, but then my little brother died from the damage to his lungs from inhaling too much smoke."

Andrea felt her heart break for the woman standing before

her as she relived the harrowing experience that cost the life of her brother.

"So yeah, it was a no-brainer for me that I would become a firefighter," she finished with an air of nonchalance.

"Celeste, I'm so sorry to hear that happened to you. I can't imagine the pain you must have battled at such a young age," Andrea sympathized.

"It's fine. I got over it," the woman replied airily.

Andrea was about to respond when she caught Donny coming her way with a man dressed in a white dress shirt, slim black tie, and navy slacks. She could see that he sported the same crests and epaulets as the other firefighters. She also noted the silver-gray hair and wrinkle lines around his eyes. She could tell that he was around her father's age, and she guessed this must be his friend, Captain Braun.

"Miss Hamilton, it is a pleasure to meet you. Lieutenant Hasgrove here was telling me that you've gotten the ball rolling already— that's what I like to hear," the captain praised as he held out his hand for her to shake.

"Thank you, Captain Braun. It is a pleasure to meet you. When you have the time, I'd like to have a sit-down with you," she requested.

"Of course. I have some free time on Thursday. I'm running out to a meeting with the fire chief now, but I'll definitely keep my Thursday free session open for you."

Andrea gave him a grateful smile before he headed back through the door.

"So, how do you like what you see?" Donny asked as he came to stand at her side.

"It's great. I like the camaraderie between your staff. They have been welcoming, and I appreciate that," she replied.

"I'm happy to hear that." Donny beamed. "They can get a bit overwhelming at times, especially if they choose to rag on you," he confessed.

She tucked a long strand of hair behind her ear before responding, "I don't mind. I can hold my own."

Andrea noticed the small smirk that graced his lips and wondered what that was about, but just then, the alarm went off.

"Lieutenant, there's an old lady stuck on the third floor of her apartment in Harbor Village. She fell and couldn't get up. Neighbors say the door is bolted from the inside."

"All right, Jay, Kevin, Sam, Celeste, Nick, you're with me. Let's go."

Andrea marveled at how quickly the firefighters sprang into action as they exited the room to head down to the trucks and grab their gear.

"Have you ever been in a fire truck before?"

Andrea stared wide-eyed at him. "No."

"Well, today is your lucky day," Donny returned, smiling down at her. "That is if you'd like to come."

"Of course," she agreed readily. "It will give me a chance to see you guys in action."

"Great. Let's go." Donny ushered her to the stairs. As they jogged down the steps, he told her, "Next time, I'll show you how to slide down the pole."

Andrea nodded excitedly, although she doubted he saw it.

"Here, put this on." Celeste handed her one of the safety jackets for her to put on.

Taking it from her hand, Andrea shrugged it on. Celeste also gave her a helmet, and she kept it by her side.

"This is called a fire truck, and the other one over there is called a fire engine," Donny informed her as he ushered her into the vehicle that had a long ladder resting at the top.

"What is the difference?" she asked, curious.

"The fire engine has all the hoses that store water. It's the main source for putting out fires. Now this one here..." Donny patted the side of the truck they were about to enter. "This one has a ladder for reaching high places that you may not be able to get in any other way. It has a number of tools for breaking, cutting, and lifting," he finished.

Andrea got to ride up front with Donny, and three of the five he had called rode in the back, and the other two followed in the ambulance.

When they made it to the apartment building, Andrea could see a crowd gathered on the outside, looking up.

"All right, Jay, I need you and Nick to head to the third floor, assess the situation, and report back to us on the ground," Donny ordered his men.

Donny and Celeste cleared the onlookers from the area they needed to position the truck. The other firefighter, Sam, remained in the truck to operate the ladder.

The guys had informed them that the lady still wasn't able to move, and Jay, who was the paramedic, predicted that her hip was broken. The door wouldn't budge, and she was too close to it for them to try to bash it in.

"All right. I'm going up."

Andrea looked to see Donny heading toward the ladder before making his way up to the window it rested against. She found herself admiring the way he took charge. He had the trait of a real alpha male.

When he disappeared through the window, he had managed to raise it without breaking it, and she finally snapped out of her troublesome thoughts.

Twenty minutes later, Donny and his team exited the entrance of the building with a lady that looked to be in her late seventies on a stretcher with a bandage over her head.

She managed to take a few photos of the scene before lowering her lens to watch Donny in action. He bent to the woman's level to hold the hand she held out to him while his mouth moved as he spoke to her. The woman nodded as he graced her with a soft smile.

The two paramedics placed her in the back of the ambulance before one stepped out and closed the doors before heading to the front to drive. Donny slapped his hand against the vehicle as it took off.

"Hey, are you okay?"

Andrea shook her head to clear it. "Oh yeah. That was amazing," she gushed.

"Thank you. It's my job," he responded, the same soft smile on his lips.

Andrea averted her eyes to calm the speeding of her heart.

"I should head home," she said anxiously.

"Of course. Sure. We're just about done here. We'll head back to the station so you can pick up your car."

Andrea gave him a grateful smile.

When they made it back to the fire station, Andrea thanked the crew for their cooperation.

"I'll be in touch," she informed Donny as he stood by the Jeep with his hands in his pockets.

As she drove off, she could see him standing by the curb, looking back at her until he was nothing but a blur.

The moment she made it home, she headed upstairs to freshen up. Her phone rang, and without hesitation, she brought it to her ear.

"Hello?"

"Hello, Miss Andrea Hamilton. This is Arthur Pennington, David Latcher's will executor. We spoke last week."

And just like that, the high she'd had from her time at the fire station plummeted from a ten to zero, and the more the man on the other end of the line spoke, the more trepidation she felt that this was the beginning of the end.

Chapter Sixteen

Andrea sat in the kitchen drinking a strong cup of coffee while she contemplated what she had to do. The call from last night had truly rattled her, and she tossed and turned in bed, barely getting any sleep. The cup she held in her hand was currently her happy place.

"Hey, you're up. Is everything okay?"

Andrea put the cup down on the counter and turned to her sister, who was standing at the kitchen door.

"I got another call from David's attorney. He says a stipulation in the will is that if Rory does not accept the conditions put forward by the end of July, then she forfeits her inheritance. So that leaves me with little to no time to tell her about the man that didn't even want her."

"Drea," Cora started sympathetically.

Andrea raised her hand, stopping her dead in her tracks.

"I know... I have to tell her. It's just this makes it even more real. I can't put it off anymore. She has to know so that she can decide if she wants to accept before it's too late." Her breath came out ragged as the thought of losing her daughter loomed greatly in her mind.

"When do you plan on telling her?" Cora asked, coming to take the seat beside her.

"She should be flying here in the next week or so. I'll tell her then," she stated.

Cora placed her hand on top of the one she had on the island and squeezed it gently. "It'll be okay, Drea, and I'll be here to help in any way I can."

Andrea turned and gave her a grateful smile.

"Enough about my problems now. How are your girls?"

At the mention of her daughters, Cora's face lit up with her smile.

"They're fine," she reported. "Julia finished her final semester for this year, and Emma is doing good. She's confident that she will be made junior associate at the advertising firm she's at soon."

"That's great. I'm happy for my nieces," Andrea replied, pleased.

She noted that Cora's expression changed slightly, and she now looked worried. Andrea gave her a questioning look.

"I'm not so sure about her relationship with her boyfriend Brian, though. She's been a bit cagey lately, and I don't know, but it just seems like something's off," she spoke in a worried voice.

Andrea nodded in understanding as she waited for her sister to continue.

"She used to tell me everything, Drea, but ever since their father's betrayal, she's been holding back a lot, and I'm worried."

At the slight tremor in Cora's voice, Andrea reached over and patted her sister's back in comfort.

"I'm sorry to hear that, Cora," she apologized. "Hopefully,

in time, she will feel comfortable enough to tell you what's really happening," she encouraged.

Cora gave Andrea a small, grateful smile as she bumped her shoulder with hers.

"Want some coffee? I made a full pot," Andrea offered.

"Yeah, sure. Thanks. I'll pour it."

Cora got up and took a mug from the cupboard to pour herself a cup.

"I'm going by the fire station this afternoon, right after I've finished painting the kitchen and bathrooms in the downstairs part of the inn with Marg," Andrea informed her sister.

"Okay," Cora acknowledged. "I'm taking Mom to her appointment today, and then I'm going grocery shopping. Is there anything you'd like me to get you?"

"No, that's fine," Andrea assured her. "Thanks, Sis."

Andrea left for the inn at the first peep of dawn to get started on applying the first coat of paint on the walls of the kitchen. She and Marg had agreed to paint the walls plain white and the cupboards Tsunami blue to give the room a bright and modern feel.

"Andrea, you started without me. Not fair."

Andrea chuckled at the fake sad puppy look the woman who'd just walked into the room was giving her.

"Hello to you, Marg," she greeted, resting the paintbrush in the container she was using.

"I thought I'd get an early start on the painting because I have quite a number of things on my agenda for today," she explained.

"Before I forget, Jamie said the painters will be available to start painting the outside by next week."

"That's great news," Andrea replied, pleased at the pace of the project. She made a note to ask Cora to work out the details for materials and labor costs with the handsome contractor that she'd been keeping at arms-length. She figured the more interaction the two got between them, the easier it would be for them to transition from friendship to something more.

"Yes, it is," Marg agreed. "The inn will be ready just in time for the influx of visitors that usually come around the end of June through September."

Curious, Andrea asked, "How many visitors are you talking about?"

"Well, by the end of June, we're usually at full capacity, and when one room empties, another gets filled."

"Wow, that's a lot. It looks like we might have to add another building," Andrea mused.

"That's a good idea," Marg replied. "Let me go change so I can come help."

Marg left to go put on some overalls while Andrea resumed her painting of the cupboards. When she returned, the two worked in unison for the next few hours. Marg left a couple of times to speak with a few of the guests that were there and explain that the kitchen was out of commission for right now. They managed to finish painting by afternoon.

"We'll have to give it another coat, possibly tomorrow, just to ensure evenness, then we can move on to the bathrooms," Andrea spoke as they gathered the paint supplies.

Andrea left to go home and freshen up and grab a bite to eat before returning to send out the emails and contact Kerry Davis, the executive social media marketing director of WeChat. The conversation she had with the woman was promising, and she left for the fire station feeling satisfied with all that she'd accomplished since the start of the day.

"Andrea, I'm glad you could make it," Donny greeted, a grin making its way onto his face.

"I'm glad too." She smiled warmly before raising her camera and snapping him unexpectedly.

"What was that for?" he asked, confused. "Are you planning to put that on the website? Please don't." At this point, his expression had changed from confusion to alarm.

Andrea laughed at this. "You can relax. I won't be putting this on the website."

She could see him visibly loosen up as his shoulders lowered, and a look of relief crossed his face.

She couldn't help the feeling to rattle him a bit more. "Not this one anyways. Who knows how many times I'll catch you by yourself unaware," she spoke matter-of-factly.

She saw him stiffen once more as he gave her a wary look. She threw her head back in laughter.

"What's so funny?" he asked, full-on perplexed by her reaction.

"The way you tensed up at the mention of getting your own photo spotlight. It's just funny," she expressed.

Donny gave her a small smile. "What can I say. I'm a simple guy. I don't really like the attention."

Andrea nodded her understanding.

"It would be nice if you allowed me to post one of these photos that I've taken of you, though. I think it would bring a level of humanness to the website and a greater appreciation of the work you all do," she expressed sincerely.

"Wait, you said photos. Does that mean you have other photos of me?" he asked, surprised.

"I have photos of all your staff both as a group and individually," she answered.

"Andrea, I appreciate that, and I'm sure the guys won't complain about being featured, but I don't really like being—"

"I just want to highlight your individual personalities and the heroes you become when you put on that suit and head out to save lives and property. You're a part of that, Donny. Why don't you want people to see what a good person you are?" she implored, looking into his sharp blue eyes staring back at her intently.

She felt an uncharacteristic warmness in her chest that seemed to be traveling up her neck and into her cheeks. She quickly averted her eyes.

"Okay," she heard him say. Her eyes found his once more as she waited for him to explain.

"You can post whatever photo you like, as long as you believe it is needed. I trust you."

At the last sentence, a wide smile graced her lips. "I promise you won't be disappointed with what I have planned."

"I know," was his simple reply.

Andrea used the time to get to know a little bit more about the staff, the types of equipment they had at the station, and how they responded to emergency calls. She even got the chance to slide down the fireman's pole that ran from the third floor where they slept when doing anywhere from twenty-four to forty-eight-hour shifts.

Her first time down, she was scared to death that she would fall off and hurt herself. She felt as if the air was being pushed out of her lungs as her heart plunged to the bottom of her stomach with the descent. When nothing major happened, she chose to go a second time and then a third. It felt exhilarating to be slicing through the air as gravity pulled her down the length of the pole.

The team responded to one medical emergency for the day, and Andrea tagged along to take a few more shots of them at work.

"Hey, Andrea. The guys are going to the Leaky Tavern. Wanna come?" Celeste asked.

She was warmed by how quickly the crew had accepted her presence at the station. She'd been coming there for the past two weeks, but she wasn't so sure it was a good idea to go out with them, seeing that after the project, she possibly wouldn't have any reason to come to the station. But she would be lying if she said she didn't enjoy their company.

"I would love to. Is that all right?" she looked to Donny for approval.

"Yes," he agreed. "You've been on two ride-alongs, so you're practically a part of the family now."

At the change of shifts, Donny left instructions with the new set of firefighters before they left for the bar. She ended up leaving her car at the station to travel with Donny and three of the firefighters.

"Hey, Gin, another round for the table," Jay, one of the four paramedics that worked at the station, called out to the bartender, who raised his hand to indicate he would soon send them over.

The group of eight had been drinking and laughing for the past hour. It was getting late, but Andrea was enjoying the company. Although she'd only had one glass of beer, she felt a little light-headed, so she nursed a glass of water instead of another drink. Donny had expressed that he didn't drink, not that he could have as he was the designated driver.

"Having a good time?" he turned to ask her.

"Yes, this is nice," she expressed with a smile.

"We're going to head out, Lieutenant. There's this place we wanna visit, but we know how much of a stick in the mud you are, so we'll see you tomorrow night."

Donny threw a straw at Sam, who had spoken. "I am not a stick in the mud," he denied. "I'm just not into your type of fun."

"Yeah, yeah. We got you, Lieutenant. Andrea, I'm happy you came; sorry we couldn't stay longer, but we should do this again," Celeste spoke, giving Andrea a side hug before sliding out of the booth.

"I'm glad too. Thanks for inviting me."

After the crew left, only Donny and Andrea remained seated in the booth.

Chapter Seventeen

"So..."

Andrea couldn't understand why she felt so nervous being alone with Donny. The awkward silence that had stretched on between them since the departure of the other firefighters was getting to her, and she needed him to say something or just call it a night and take her back to her Jeep.

"So..." he echoed, seemingly as nervous as she. "How does it feel to be back in Oak Harbor?" he asked eventually.

Andrea looked at him, surprised. "How did you know I just came back to Oak Harbor?" she asked, raising an eyebrow.

Donny scratched the back of his neck. "Well, I asked Captain Braun about you, and he told me you moved back after your father's death. I hope you don't mind," he spoke sheepishly.

"No, it's fine." She smiled. "It saves me the time of me explaining why we've never met before a week ago."

"True," he agreed.

"What else did the captain tell you about me?" she asked, curious.

Donny shrugged. "Not much, really, just that you have two other sisters and that you're a big deal in the social media field."

Andrea chuckled. "So basically not much then," she quantified.

"I guess not," Donny returned. "Why don't you tell me something more about yourself. Any pets, kids?"

"No pets. I did have a Labradoodle a few years back, but he died, and I didn't get around to having another pet. I just couldn't bear going through such a loss again."

"I'm sorry to hear that," Donny expressed.

She could see the sincerity in his eyes.

"Thanks... I do have a daughter, though. She's my pride and joy." A smile broke out at the mention of her daughter. "She's the best thing that has ever happened to me, and I don't know what I would do if I ever lost her," she confessed, the weight of her words causing a sinking feeling in her chest.

"I know what you mean," Donny offered, causing her to raise her head to see the knowing look he gave her. "I have two sons. I can't imagine ever losing them," he revealed.

Andrea grinned.

"I have pictures. Would you like to see them?" he asked.

"Of course."

Donny reached for his wallet and flipped it open. "This is Trey; he's nineteen. He wants to become a fireman, but I wanted him to go to college, so the compromise is he's taking a few courses at the community college on Pioneer Way."

"You're talking about Skagit Valley College?" she asked.

"He'll do the two years, and then if he still wants to be a firefighter, I promised him I wouldn't stand in his way."

"That's a good compromise," Andrea agreed.

Donny gave her a smile of gratitude before pointing to another photo of a young man that looked like a younger version of himself. "This is Bruce. He's twenty-two, married, and they're expecting their first child in six months."

"Wow, that's great. You're going to be a grandpa," Andrea spoke, all the while cheesing.

"Yeah, it's so surreal. One minute they're wearing diapers, you're cleaning scraped knees, seeing them off to college, and then they're starting a family. It still feels like they just came into the world to me," he pondered.

Andrea raised her chin, understanding his words. "It does. My daughter's engaged to be married, and yet I still see her as my little baby that I need to protect at all cost," she confessed.

"A parent's job is never done, even after they've left the nest," he offered.

The two remained at the bar a full hour after the others had left, just talking about their children and any random thing that came to their minds. They drank the last of their drinks and then made their way out of the bar and headed home.

"I had a great time tonight... you know, despite the rocky start we had," Andrea told Donny while they stood on the front porch.

"You mean bumpy," he injected with a laugh.

The sound was so deep and rich as it shook his frame, and the mirth drew her in.

"You're right." She chortled. "Let's never do that again, though."

"Never," Donny conceded as his shining eyes stayed fixed on her.

"As much as I'm thankful you brought me home, you know I could have driven myself," she spoke, breaking the tension.

"I wouldn't feel comfortable letting you drive home after keeping you out so long and with the one drink you had..." Donny shook his head. "I know it might not be enough to cloud your judgment, but to someone else, it makes a big difference," he stated seriously.

"Speaking from experience?" she asked, sensing there was a story there.

Donny's lips pursed together as a haunted look passed through his eyes.

"My wife, she was killed in a car accident... the other driver he... he was distracted. He lost control, and his car ended up in the lane where the cars were traveling in the opposite direction. By the time my wife saw what was happening, it was too late... it was a head-on collision, and the impact killed her on the spot."

"Oh my God!" Andrea exclaimed as her heart slammed against her chest with the despair she felt for Donny. "I'm so sorry, Donny. I can't imagine how you could have got through that." Andrea placed her hand on his arm, offering her support.

"Now I'm really sorry for how I behaved toward you during the accident. I was so insensitive, and it was my fault," she babbled on, feeling the guilt seeping up from her actions.

"Is that the only reason you're sorry now?"

"No, I was sorry bef—" She stopped mid-sentence when she saw the glint in his eyes.

"I know. I'm just getting you back for earlier today." He smirked.

"That's not fair." She pouted. "This is a serious issue."

"I know," Donny replied. "I know you're sorry, too, but that man was also drunk, so don't feel guilty. I realized that you were going through a lot," he reassured her.

After Donny left, she went upstairs and took a shower. When she entered her bedroom, her cell was ringing. Picking it up, she realized it was her daughter. Her heart squeezed against her chest.

"Hi, sweetheart. How are you?" she managed to breathe out.

"Hi, Mom. I'm fine. Why do you sound like that? Is everything okay?" Rory asked in concern.

"I'm fine, sweetie. I'm just a little tired. I had a long day," she spoke apologetically. She was relieved that it seemed no one had gotten to her daughter before she was able to speak with her, but she was also anxious about the repercussions that were sure to follow her confessing.

"How are you doing?" she changed the subject.

"I'm fine, Mom. Guess who is now officially an associate at Smart, Pleck & Gamble LLC?"

"Awesome! James won his case," Andrea cheesed, happy for her son-in-law. She knew how hard he'd worked to pass the bar and become a lawyer, and now that he had been made a permanent fixture at the law firm that had been his dream, she couldn't be happier for him.

"Yeah, Mom, he did," Rory said excitedly.

"I'm proud of him. I'm happy for you both," she congratulated.

"Thanks, Mom. I know James appreciates your support. I was actually calling to let you know that since he wrapped up his case so quickly, we'll be visiting Oak Harbor next week. We bought the tickets already. Keep your fingers crossed that they don't throw another case his way too soon because of his big win."

"That's wonderful, sweetheart. I can't wait to see you both," Andrea replied as her heart beat erratically against her chest. Her anxiety had just reached a new level with her daughter's announcement.

"Seriously, Mom, you don't sound too well. Maybe you should go lie down for a bit," Rory encouraged out of concern.

"Maybe you're ... you're right. I'm going to lie down for a bit."

"Okay, Mom, I'll talk to you later. I hope you feel better after you get some rest," Rory expressed.

"Thanks, sweetie. I'll speak to you later."

After the two hung up, Andrea sat on her bed and placed her head in her hands as she leaned over, feeling overwhelmed.

After some time of sitting in the same position, she got up, threw on a robe, and went downstairs to the kitchen. She opened the freezer and removed the large tub of chocolate fudge brownie Ben & Jerry's ice cream before setting it on the kitchen island and getting a spoon from the drawer. Andrea dug into the sweet confection, willing all her troubles away.

"I know that look," her mother said, walking into the kitchen.

Andrea put the spoon back into the ice cream as she looked up at her mother guiltily. "Hey, Mom," she greeted lowly.

"What's got you eating comfort food at two a.m. in the morning, sweetie?" Becky queried, coming to sit across from her.

Andrea went to put the cover back on the ice cream when her mother swiped the container from before her and held out her hand for the spoon.

"It's nothing, Mom. I'll handle it," she assured Becky, not wanting to burden her with her problems, knowing that she was carrying her own burdens from her illness.

"Drea..." Andrea looked over at her mother from the seriousness in her tone. "I'm your mother, don't shut me out," she pleaded.

"Mom..." Andrea sighed. "I don't want to burden you with my problems when you have..." she trailed off, leaving the weight of what she left unsaid in the air.

"Yes, I have ALS, but that doesn't give you girls the right to treat me like an invalid. I am your mother," Becky finished strongly. "I just want the chance to be your mother the way I didn't get to be for twenty-four years," she continued.

Andrea could hear the hurt and pain behind her mother's words, and her heart broke for her.

"I know, Mom." Andrea ran her palm soothingly against

the back of her mother's hand. "I'm sorry if I made you feel like you don't matter because you do, and I really need your advice."

Becky flipped her hand over and held her daughter's in an act of strength.

"Remember when I told you all those years ago when you visited me back in New York that Rory's father died?"

"Mm-hmm," Becky replied.

"Well... I lied," she confessed, ducking her eyes away from her mother.

"Drea," her mother breathed out in shock.

"I know, Mom. I shouldn't have lied, but Rory's father didn't want anything to do with her, and I didn't want my daughter growing up believing that she was unwanted...that she was a mistake," she expressed as tears began pooling in her eyes.

"Oh, sweetie, I'm so sorry that you had to go through that," Becky replied in a pained voice. She rushed over to hug her tightly against her chest as Andrea's tears fell unhindered.

"It was the worst experience I've had, Mom; even worse than Dad turning his back on me," she cried.

Becky lovingly ran her hand over her daughter's hair as she clung to her and released the pain she'd had inside for so long.

"I was so lost, and I didn't know what to do. I wanted to come home, but then I remembered what Dad said, and I was young and stupid and proud..."

"Shh, sweetie, it's not your fault. We should have been there more for you, girls. I should have been there more." Becky cupped her daughter's face in her hands as she looked into her tear-filled eyes. "I am proud of you for being strong for yourself and your daughter when no one else was there to be strong for you both," she soothed her daughter.

Andrea beamed at her mother through her tears, comforted by her words.

"Thanks, Mom," she replied in gratitude.

Becky gave her a warm smile before placing a kiss on her forehead.

After Andrea had finally calmed, she was ready to tell her what the problem was.

"He died... Rory's father and he's left something for her. I'm not sure what, though. The lawyer says she has to accept the terms by the end of July. I don't know how to tell her this, and I'm scared I'll lose her if I do tell her," she admitted.

"Drea, you have to tell her," Becky stated. "You need to tell Aurora, or this will haunt you for the rest of your life, and if she finds out any other way than from you, then you stand a greater chance of losing her. Just be honest and tell her why you didn't want her to know."

Andrea listened to her mother's words, stating the inevitable, and yet still, she couldn't help but wish she would have given her a different response.

"She might get angry and resent you for keeping the truth from her, but you're still her mother... the one who has been there all of her life. Nothing can beat that love. She will still love you, Drea, have faith."

"If I've never said it before, I love you, Mom," she expressed.

"I love you, too, Drea," Becky replied, bringing Andrea into her embrace.

"This is a wonderful sight to see, but now I'm jealous. Where's my hug?"

The two pulled apart. Turning, they saw Cora standing at the kitchen entrance with a pout on her lips, but the glint in her eyes suggested it wasn't serious.

Suddenly she burst out in laughter, and the others followed suit.

Chapter Eighteen

Andrea couldn't believe that three weeks had already passed, and she was pleased with all the work she'd accomplished. Last week she and Marg had finished painting and wallpapering the kitchen and bathrooms. Marg had convinced her to paint the room she took for her office to maintain uniformity. The new furniture for the lobby had arrived, but they decided not to put them out until the area had been painted. The paints had arrived, and it was now just a matter of waiting on the workmen to finish painting the building so that they could put them out.

She'd also visited the fire station every day after she finished her own work. She had enough to begin designing the new website, but if she was honest, she liked being at the fire station and getting the opportunity just to watch them all in action.

Cora had made a sly comment that it seemed she'd found a new family, but she didn't take the bait. She was just doing her job, and the time was just a bonus... for now.

"Hi, Andrea."

Andrea looked up from the pictures she was scanning on the camera to see Celeste standing before her.

"Hey, Celeste," she greeted back. "What's on your mind?"

She noted that the other firefighters in the lounge kept throwing furtive looks over at them, and she wondered what that was about.

"We're having a cookout this Saturday at Captain Braun's house. Most of the staff will be attending along with some of their family members," she rambled on. "All the guys are going to be there, and we were wondering if you'd like to come as Lieutenant Hasgrove's plus one."

Andrea looked at the woman wide-eyed.

"I don't think that's a good idea," she started to decline.

"Oh, come on, Andrea, it'll be fun. I promise, and you're invited because you're practically a part of the family. We've already claimed you, so you can't say no," Celeste stated.

Andrea hesitated. She would love to go to the cookout, but she didn't want to give them the wrong idea that something was developing between their lieutenant and her.

"Guys, back me up here," Celeste threw over her shoulders.

"It'll be fun," Jay called out.

"We promise to be on our best behavior; Scout's honor," Nick chimed in, making the sign of the cross.

Andrea snorted at their goofiness.

"Captain Braun would appreciate you being there, and Lieutenant Hasgrove. Right, Donny?"

Andrea turned toward where Celeste was looking to see Donny stepping through the entrance. Donny stopped in his tracks and furrowed his brows in confusion.

"I was telling Andrea that you would appreciate her presence at Cap's cookout," Celeste quickly filled him in.

Donny's gaze quickly cut to Andrea, who was already

staring at him before staring back at Celeste and then back to her. Andrea caught movement from her periphery, and she wondered what the other woman was doing. Just as she made to turn her head, Donny spoke up.

"I mean, if you want to come, we'd all be happy to have you," he spoke with a small unsure smile. "No pressure, though."

"When you put it like that, how could I resist," Andrea replied, giving him a small grin before cutting her gaze back to Celeste, who was punching the air as if she'd just won a prize.

Andrea gave her a quizzical look.

"I'm just happy not to be the only female representative from the department at these shindigs," she explained.

"But I'm not a member of the department." Andrea released a light chuckle.

The woman said something under her breath, and Andrea wondered what it was that caused Celeste to look at her with so much hope.

"All right, guys, stop pestering Andrea. She already said yes. If you continue being so creepy, she just might change her mind," Donny chided his team.

"Yes, sir," the team echoed in unison, giving a half salute before breaking out in laughter.

Andrea shook her head in amusement.

Donny gave her an apologetic smile, but she waved him off.

* * *

On the day of the barbecue, Andrea couldn't decide what to wear even though Donny would be there to pick her up within the next half hour. She'd spent most of the time since she woke contemplating her outfit and overall appearance. She didn't want to overdress, but at the same time, she didn't want to be underdressed. She'd asked him what the dress code for the cookout was, but he had simply told her to dress comfortably.

"How comfortable?" she'd asked.

"I'm not sure how to answer that," he replied, giving her a confused look.

She looked down at the white sleeveless sundress with floral prints, the black denim pants and white blouse ensemble, and the patterned maxi dress, which confused her all the more. She was clearly undecided. Maybe she should just wear a simple T-shirt and some shorts, she thought.

"Drea, what are you doing? Your date will be here any minute," Cora asked as she stepped into her room.

She released a defeated exhale. "I can't decide what to wear," she admitted. "And he's not my date— we're not going on a date. He's just escorting me to the cookout where all the firefighters will be," she rationalized.

Cora raised a skeptical brow. "If you say so..."

Andrea sighed, exasperated by her sister's efforts to play matchmaker.

"Think whatever you like. This is not a date," she finished with finality. "Now, can you help me choose an outfit before Donny gets here?" she pleaded.

Cora smirked before coming to stand over her clothing selection.

"Wear the sundress," she suggested. "You can never go wrong with that."

Andrea quickly stepped into the outfit. She chose to wear her hair down in loose curls, so all she had left to do was spritz some of her vanilla-scented body spray at her neck and behind her ears and apply some gloss to her lips. She then stepped into her low-heeled, thong sandals.

"You look beautiful, Sis," Cora complimented. "If you were going to prom, I would have had to snap a picture of you and your date."

"Cora," Andrea snapped in warning.

She held up her hands in surrender. Just then, they heard the doorbell. Grabbing her purse, Andrea made her way downstairs, with Cora following closely behind.

"Well, hello there," Donny said with a charming smile as soon as the door opened.

"Hi," she returned. She was surprised at how breathy her voice sounded.

"Hi, I'm Cora, Drea's sister," she greeted, holding her hand out.

"A pleasure to meet you," he replied, accepting the hand Cora held out to him.

"It's a pleasure to meet you too, Donny," Cora returned. "This is nice. Andrea met my friend that I made when I just moved here, and now, I'm meeting her new friend," Cora stated cryptically.

Donny gave her a puzzled look, but Andrea stepped in front of her sister, preventing her from embarrassing her.

"Let's go." Hooking her arm under his, she steered him off the porch and toward his car.

"Bye Drea, bye Donnie. Have fun."

Andrea rolled her eyes at her sister's mischief while Donny chuckled in amusement.

"Your sister is something else," Donny spoke as they drove off the property.

"She's something all right," she seethed.

"I can tell that she really loves you, though."

Andrea looked over at him with a smile. "I know."

When they arrived at Captain Braun's house, Andrea felt her palms sweating from anxiety.

"Relax," Donny soothed her. "You know almost everyone that will be here. They won't make you feel uncomfortable, I promise."

As soon as they entered the house, she was greeted by the

captain's bubbly wife, who gushed over the dress she wore, wishing she was a couple of decades younger and a few pounds less to pull it off.

When she made it out to the backyard, it was the same energy. Everyone welcomed her cheerfully, and she was involved in their conversations as she'd always been coming to their cookouts.

"Excuse me, ladies, but can I steal Andrea for a while?"

"Of course," Celeste readily agreed, smiling broadly.

Andrea looked up to see Donny smiling down at her with an outstretched hand. She put her hand in his and allowed him to help her up.

"I want to introduce you to my sons," he informed her as he guided her to another section of the yard.

He led her over to two young men who were laughing at whatever the female that stood by the older one holding her protectively was saying.

"Trey, Bruce, Janice," Donny spoke up, getting their attention. "This is Andrea Hamilton. She's the one restructuring our website."

Bruce and Janice gave her a broad smile as they held out their hands for her to shake. "It's a pleasure to meet you, Ms. Hamilton. Dad has told us a lot about you," Bruce said.

"All good things, I hope," she replied, turning her head to Donny in question. "And please call me Andrea." The couple nodded in acceptance.

"Trey," she heard Donny say in what seemed to be a gruff whisper.

Andrea turned to the younger son just as he turned from whatever battle he and his father were having.

"It's a pleasure to meet you, Andrea," he said with a polite smile.

Andrea could feel the tension rolling off his body and knew the sentiments he expressed were possibly far from the truth.

"Likewise," she replied simply, shaking his hand.

"I'm gonna go talk to Chelsea," he said, excusing himself.

"I'm sorry, Andrea. He isn't good with meeting new people," Donny apologized as he brought her back over to the group of women she was with previously.

"It's fine, I understand," she replied.

Donny excused himself, and she spent the next fifteen minutes talking and laughing with the wives and girlfriends of the other firefighters, with her and Celeste being the exception.

Andrea excused herself from the group to go use the restroom. On her way out of the house, she could hear voices that seemed to be arguing out on the back porch.

"It's like you're trying to replace Mom like our feelings don't matter..."

"That's not fair."

Andrea stopped herself from pushing open the back door.

"I'll always love your mother, and no one can possibly take her place. No one will..."

Andrea retraced her steps but headed for the front door. She couldn't listen anymore. She wasn't sure why Donny's words affected her as they did, but as he spoke, it felt as if someone had used a knife to puncture whatever high she was on.

"She means nothing to me. I want us to work. I promise I'll stop behaving like a bachelor for you. Jus-just give me another chance."

The tears streamed down her face as she watched the man who she thought was falling in love with her drive the final nail in her coffin as he tried to salvage the relationship with the female she had no clue about.

Just like that, Andrea realized that she was always on the losing side in the game of love.

"Andrea, are you okay?"

"Can you take me home, please? I'm-I'm not feeling well,

and I don't want to bother Donny. He needs to spend time with his family."

Celeste nodded in understanding while her eyes shone with her concern.

"Okay, let me just get my stuff, then we can go."

Andrea gave her a grateful smile.

"Drea, Celeste said you weren't feeling well." Donny came through the front door.

She winced. This was the first time he had called her by her nickname, and it felt as if he had burned her.

"Yeah. I'm just gonna go. I don't want to ruin the fun," she replied as lightly as she could.

"Hey. Ready to go?" Celeste interrupted whatever Donny was about to say.

"I can take you back. It wouldn't be any trouble," he offered.

"No," she spoke up. "You should stay here with your family."

Donny agreed, but from the look on his face, she knew he wanted to say more.

"Ready," she informed Celeste, turning and heading toward the car.

"Are you sure it wasn't something someone said?" Celeste asked in a worried tone as she sped along Torpedo Road toward Andrea's home.

"No," she lied, leaning her head against the car glass and willing herself to forget the words she heard Donny speak.

"All right, if you say so," Celeste replied in a skeptical tone. "Just know that if it was something someone said, I've got your back," she assured her.

Andrea gave the woman who was over five inches taller than her a grateful smile. "I know," she confirmed.

Andrea warily walked up the steps of the front porch,

feeling completely depleted, and it wasn't from being out in the sun too long. Just as she reached for the knob, the door flew open, and her daughter stood on the other side.

"Surprise!"

Chapter Nineteen

"Surprise, Mom!"

"Rory," Andrea managed to squeeze out even though it felt as if all the air had left her body.

Rory wrapped her arms around her mother, but the warmth emanating from her couldn't chase the chills running up and down Andrea's spine.

"What on earth are you doing here? I thought you said you guys couldn't make it again."

"It's just me," Rory revealed. "James's case is still in the early stages, so he can't travel, but after the last two attempts to come here to visit you and realizing it may not be possible for us to travel together for a while, he convinced me to come, and so here I am," she explained. "But judging from your reaction, I would say you're not happy I'm here," she observed.

"No, I'm happy... Of course, I'm happy, honey. You just took me off guard. I've missed you." Andrea mustered a smile she hoped was bright enough to hide the panic attack she was having. "It's just that I went out, and it didn't go as expected, and I'm not feeling well."

"Oh yeah, Aunt Cora told me you were on a date. What happened?" Rory enquired, going into full worry mode.

"It wasn't a date, and it's nothing," she said nonchalantly.

"Are you sure?" Rory asked, unconvinced. "Because earlier you weren't feeling well."

"I think it was the sun. I was out in the sun too long."

"Then you should go lie down, Mom. We can catch up when you're feeling better."

"Okay, sweetie," she agreed, lightly cupping her daughter's cheek before releasing it and heading upstairs.

As soon as she stepped through the door of her room, she crumpled on the floor while dry heaving. She hadn't felt a panic attack as intense in a while, and it took all her energy to crawl toward her desk to remove the paper bag of sweets, then empty the content before bringing the bag to her mouth and breathing in and out to calm down.

Shortly after she managed to pull herself onto her bed, there was a knock at the door, and Cora pushed her head through.

"Rory said you weren't feeling well," she said softly as she stepped into the room and closed the door.

"Oh my God, Cora, what am I going to do?" she asked, crumpling the bag in her hand.

Cora walked over to her sister at sat beside her on the bed. "You have to tell her, Drea," she implored. "Before it's too late and you lose her forever."

Andrea exhaled as her sister's words sank in.

"How long before the clause in the will expires?"

"The end of this month," Andrea replied weakly.

Cora sucked in her breath. "Drea, that's less than three weeks away. You will have to muster the courage to tell her, both for hers and your sake."

"I will," Andrea promised. "After the barbecue."

"Drea—"

"After the barbecue," she reiterated.

Cora sighed but chose to give up on the topic for now. "What happened at the cookout? I thought you would be there until at least evening."

At this, Andrea groaned. "Yeah, that was the plan, but then I overheard Donny talking to his son about me never being able to take the place of his dead wife, and I don't know... I guess something just broke in me, and I just couldn't stay," she confessed.

Cora gave her a sympathetic look. "You really liked him, don't you?"

"No...yes...maybe...I don't know." She exhaled. "I wasn't looking to get involved in a relationship with him, and based on his response, he wasn't looking for one either. Now that's resolved, I can go back to doing what I was hired for."

Cora patted her back but didn't offer any words of advice.

"I have once again been reminded to never mix business with pleasure."

Her phone buzzed, and she lifted it to see that a text message had come in from Donny.

Donny: How are you feeling?

Andrea: I'm much better. Thanks for the concern.

Donny: ...Okay

She noted that the three little dots blinked in and out of the text box as if he was struggling to type something.

Andrea: Goodnight.

With that, she put her phone on Do Not Disturb and turned to her bed. Perhaps that nap wasn't so bad after all.

Andrea spent the next few days going up and down with her daughter to visit the various sites the island had to offer. She took her to Deception Pass State Park, and they had the time of their lives. They visited the old library, surprised to find that Mrs. Debra Nunes was still the Librarian there. They also went to the bakery owned by Kerry. Rory got to sample the cakes she had. She had nothing but praise for the woman's skills, and Andrea couldn't agree more.

She arranged for Rory to meet a few of her aunts and cousins so that she wouldn't feel awkward among them during the barbecue that was only a week away.

They had put off having Fourth of July celebrations because, at the time, most of the family wouldn't have been available to attend, but now everyone was available for July seventeenth.

She'd only been back to the station four times after what happened at the captain's house, and though she still rapped well with the staff, she maintained a professional relationship with Donny.

The website was almost complete. She just needed a few more photos of the staff in full uniform, and they were planning on having a parade close to the end of August. After that, she would be finished with the Oak Harbor Fire Department and its members, one in particular that she was trying at all costs to stay clear of.

"Sweetie, I'm heading down to the station, then I'm going to the store. Do you need anything?"

"No, Mom. I'm fine," Rory assured her, lazing on her bed. Rory had wanted to take a room at the inn, but she'd managed to get her to just stay in her room, and she was reveling in the closeness.

Very soon, this would all be gone, she thought, replaced by hurt and accusations and possibly Rory not being able to wait to be as far away as she could get from her. She shivered at the thought.

"Okay. I'll be back in a few."

* * *

"Andrea, can I speak with you for a minute?"

Andrea looked up to see Donny beckoning to her.

"Excuse me, guys," she spoke to the two paramedics who had been explaining the level of training they had to go through as medics that worked with this department as opposed to those who worked for hospitals and medical centers.

Donny walked to his office, and she followed him there and allowed him to usher her in.

"What's going on, Andrea?" he asked, getting straight to the point.

"What do you mean?" she asked, feigning ignorance.

"You know what," he cried out exasperated. "Ever since the cookout, you've been distant, treating me like a leper, and I would like to know why. I thought we were at least friends."

Andrea sighed before fixing serious eyes on him.

"We're not friends, Donny."

Donny pulled his head back as if she'd slapped him while he stared wide-eyed at her.

"At least we can't be friends. Not when it threatens the relationship you have with your sons and the memory of your wife. I can't, and I wouldn't want to replace her," she revealed.

Donny cursed under his breath as it dawned on him that she'd heard the conversation he'd had with his son.

"How much did you hear?" he asked with arms folded across his chest.

"Enough," she stated, "to know that I wouldn't want to come between you and the bond you have with your sons."

"Drea, please just let me explain," he implored.

There... he called her Drea again. Her heartbeat picked up its pace, and she waited for him to speak.

"Trey is wary of anyone he doesn't truly know. He always has been, and with the death of his mom, it compacted the issue," he explained. "He just needs some time to get to know you, and I know he would change his mind."

"What makes you so sure he would?" she asked skeptically.

"Because he would be seeing the vibrant, quirky, loyal, and beautiful person that stands before me with a heart of gold," he stated.

Andrea looked at him, startled by his comment. Her fingernails dug into her palms as her breathing became rattled. She needed to get a grip on her emotions. Averting her eyes, she willed the resolve back.

"I understand what you're saying, but for now, we can't be friends, more like associates. I have my own relationship with my daughter that I need to work out, and that has to take priority above everything else right now. I can't be worrying whether or not one of your sons likes me. I just can't."

"Okay," Donny replied, holding up his hands in acceptance.

On the drive to the supermarket, Andrea failed at keeping her thoughts off Donny, at the hurt reflected in his blue eyes after she told him they couldn't be friends. She knew she made the right decision, but why did it feel as if she'd lost an important part of her person. Shaking the feeling, she continued on her journey.

On the day of the barbecue, Andrea sat comfortably in one of the bamboo chairs on the patio, holding the orange cushion to her chest as her laughter shook her whole frame.

Her cousin Brian had made it to the barbecue along with Kirsten and their two children, Mitch and Nikki. He was telling her how an old lady had driven him down to cuss him out for littering the road when in fact, all he had done was put out one of the roadwork signs to alert passengers that they would have to take a detour because that section of the road was being fixed.

"I kid you not. She was like, young man—"

Andrea bellowed at the high-pitched, squeaky voice her cousin was imitating.

"—don't you know it is a crime to litter the streets with your garbage? I should report you to the local authorities, but I'll just let you off with a warning. Don't. Ever. Do. It. Again."

Andrea nearly slid off the chair, and her mirth brought tears to her eyes. Rory, who sat to her left, held her hand and squeezed as the laughter became too much for her. She ended up wheezing as she tried to catch her breath.

"Brian, this is too hilarious. Please, no more right now. Let me catch my breath first," Andrea begged, even as her body shook with the tremors of her dying laughter.

"All right, Drea, but I'm telling you, the things I witness working for the city makes me treasure my crazy family even more. There are some real crazy people out there that can make you question what percentage of the population is actually sane."

"The food's ready!" Uncle Luke called loudly enough for those out by the picnic table and wandering about could hear.

"Yes!" Josh, Ben's son, cheered.

Soon everyone was lining up at the grill to choose from the varying meat choices available. Music played in the background while the family sat and ate and talked.

"Jo!" Andrea heard Kerry call out.

She looked toward the porch to see her sister coming down the stairs toward the gathering. Her heart soared with happiness. This day could not get any better.

Andrea got up and walked over to her sister, who was being tightly embraced by Kerry. After they separated, Andrea pulled her sister to her in a crushing hug.

"I'm happy you're here, Jo Jo," she spoke excitedly.

"Me too, Drea," her sister reciprocated.

Cora was the next one to greet Josephine, and Andrea was satisfied by their interaction. She could see that Josephine was making an effort to move past the resentment she once felt toward their older sister.

144

After the others greeted Josephine, they finally got the chance to sit and continue enjoying the barbecue.

The family didn't leave until late in the evening. Andrea and Rory sat on the porch swing in comfort, listening to the sounds of the night. Andrea took a sip from the glass of merlot she held in her hand. She relished the peace and tranquility of just sitting with her daughter with no words being exchanged, but she knew that was about to come to an end with what she needed to say next.

"Aurora."

"Yeah, Mom, what is it?" Rory asked on alert as her mother had used her by her full name.

Andrea turned to look at her daughter with a sad smile.

"My sweet, sweet Aurora." She reached out to touch her daughter's ginger hair before cupping her face and placing a gentle kiss on her cheek.

"Mom, you're scaring me," Rory spoke, her voice shaking with fear.

"I'm so sorry, sweetie. For everything."

Rory looked at her mother with furrowed brows.

"I want you to know that what I'm about to tell you... I only did it to protect you."

"Mom," Rory returned, her voice quaking.

"Your father didn't die when you were a baby. I lied... he just passed away last month, and he left an inheritance for you. In order to claim the inheritance, you must acknowledge it by the end of this month," she rushed out.

"What?"

Andrea's gaze was glued to her daughter's. She watched as Aurora's face was marred with confusion and tried to let the information sink in, but Andrea knew once it did, anger would be the next emotion to take over. She gulped down the remaining remnants of her wine for support.

She knew she was going to need it.

Chapter Twenty

If a pin had been dropped in that instant, the distinct clinking sound would have been heard without much effort. Neither said anything as they stared at each other, Andrea with eyes of regret and Rory with wide eyes.

"What?" she echoed again, shooting off the swing.

"I know it's a lot to take in, sweetie, but please just let me explain to you what happened so you can understand," Andrea reasoned with her daughter.

"You kept this from me my entire life. How could you be so selfish?" Rory returned with a guttural cry.

"I know. I'm sorry, Rory. Please let me just explain—"

Rory held up her hand, halting whatever her mother was about to say.

"I can't be around you right now," Rory shot before she turned and ran off the porch and into the darkness.

"Rory!" Andrea stood and called after her daughter, but she just kept going.

Andrea collapsed on the swing as her tears racked her body. She felt overwhelmed by her sadness and helplessness. She stayed on the porch until after midnight, but Rory still hadn't come back, causing her to worry that something had happened to her. That feeling was replaced by relief when Cora came out to tell her that Rory had decided to take a room at the inn. She also felt disappointed that she didn't come back so they could talk it over, but she knew she had to give her daughter space to come to terms with her betrayal.

"You need to get some sleep, Drea. It doesn't make sense to punish yourself any more than what you're experiencing now," Cora implored even as she ran her hand over her hair as she lay in her lap.

"I lost her, Cora. I lost my daughter," she sobbed.

"Drea, she'll come around. She just needs time to process all that she's been told," Josephine spoke from the other end of the swing as she rubbed Andrea's leg that lay across her lap.

"Come on. Let's go inside. I'll make you a cup of chamomile tea. Maybe that'll help you sleep," Cora offered.

"It's fine. I just want to go lie down," she returned.

The sisters stayed in her room until fatigue won out, and she finally fell asleep. When she awoke, the sun was peeking through the opening of her curtains. Andrea swung her legs that felt like lead over the edge of the bed and willed herself to get up and get ready.

When she made it downstairs, she realized that her sister had left breakfast out for her. She only managed a few sips of coffee and a couple of bites of the egg and bacon before the queasiness in her stomach won out.

She decided to go for a walk and possibly stop by the rose garden in the back. The back door was slightly ajar, and as she made her way to it, she heard voices on the porch.

"...but she lied to me, Grandma, how... how do I forgive her for this? How do we get past this? I feel like my whole life has been a lie."

Andrea covered her mouth to stem the sobs that emanated from her as her daughter's words hit her like a sack of bricks.

"You forgive her because she is your mother and because in all this time, she has loved you unconditionally like no one else could," was her mother's reply.

"But she lied to me."

"Let me ask you something. Do you think your mother would do anything, and I mean anything at all, to intentionally hurt you?"

"Well... no," Rory stated. "Not until now, that is."

"Okay, that's fair, but could there be a reason that she would deliberately keep this from you?"

"I guess to spare my feelings, or it could have been to spite my father... to get back at him."

Andrea found herself looking through the door at her mother and daughter as they sat on the long couch.

"How will you know if you don't let her explain?"

"I'm just so angry at her right now," Rory confessed.

"I know you are, honey, but please give her a chance. You only get one mother."

"All right, Grandma, I will."

"That's my girl," Becky replied, bopping her chin with her finger.

Andrea's heart warmed at the gesture and at their bonding, even as her tears ran freely down her cheeks as her own predicament loomed over her. She quickly made her way back inside when she realized that they were finished talking and could catch her standing there at any minute.

Her mother came through the kitchen door, and Andrea immediately flew into her arms.

Becky rubbed her hand over her daughter's hair as she allowed her to cry against her shoulder and receive any strength she was able to give her.

"Thank you, Mom. It really means a lot to me that you spoke with her."

"Any time, sweetie," Becky replied. "Just give her some time. She will come around."

* * *

"Enjoy your picnic," Andrea encouraged her sister, who was currently heading out the door to greet the tall, handsome gentleman that stood there.

"Thanks, Sis. I will," Cora promised.

She was happy to see her sister's love life take off as it had a rocky start, but it was going good now. She didn't feel uncomfortable taking their relationship public now as she had in the beginning. She could see that Jamie treated her like a princess and that Cora had become completely enamored by him. She was happy that her sister had found love after the dissolution of her marriage

Andrea stood back admiring the beautifully painted inn. The mustard yellow perfectly complemented the white-framed windows and the wraparound porches, all painted white.

"Beautiful, isn't it?" Marg asked as she stood beside her.

"Yup, that it is. They did a great job."

They did indeed do a great job, and everything had come together nicely, from the lobby being painted royal blue and the bedrooms having their own color scheme.

"It all came together nicely."

"Speaking of nice..."

Andrea turned to look at what had caught Marg's attention to see Donny making purposeful steps toward her.

Her heart rate picked up its pace as she stood in position, waiting.

"Hello, ladies," he greeted with a large smile.

"Hello, to you too," Marg replied, holding out her hand.

Donny shook it and smiled at her before turning his gaze back to Andrea.

"I'll be inside," Marg offered up.

"Actually, I just need to get a few things. Please excuse me for a minute," she expressed to Donny, who gave her a slight nod.

Andrea quickly grabbed her laptop and the files she needed before heading back out.

"I wasn't sure you had gotten my message," Andrea spoke sheepishly. She'd sent him an email asking him to meet her by the family's restaurant to go over a few things for the website before it was relaunched when he was available earlier today. It surprised her that he made it there just a few hours later.

Donny raised his hand to scratch the back of his head. "I did. You didn't state a time, so..."

Andrea looked at him apologetically.

"I should have stated a time. I'm sorry about that."

"No worries," he replied. "Shall we?" he asked, gesturing in the direction of the restaurant.

Andrea walked beside Donny in awkward silence. She itched to say something, anything to break the tension that kept the unseen chasm between them. She missed how easy it used to be to talk to him, but for the sake of preservation, it was best they didn't converse too much. She didn't want to be the reason his relationship with his son became strained. As soon as this project was wrapped up, they could go their separate ways and forget they had ever crashed into each other.

Donny held the door for Andrea, allowing her to walk into the cavernous space. A few tables were filled with the inn's guests and a few walk-ins for the lunch hour.

Kay, another of the bubbly waitresses, led them to a seat closer to the back. Donny pulled out Drea's seat, and she thanked him as she sat.

"Would you like to order now?" the petite young woman asked, her writing pad perched to take their order.

"Not for me, thanks, Kay," Andrea declined before turning to Donny, waiting for him to decide if he wanted to order anything.

"I am a bit famished, but I would feel better ordering if you'd let me get something for you," he spoke. "You can order anything you like. I won't mind."

Andrea raised a brow at him. "You do realize that I practically own this restaurant, right?"

"I know," he acknowledged, "but I would appreciate it if you would accept my offer. It's my way of showing you that chivalry isn't dead."

"I can come back when you have decided," the waitress chimed in after standing there observing their discomfort.

"No," Andrea replied, "I'll order. I'm taking up Mr. Hasgrove here on his offer."

The smile that made its way onto Donny's face made it look as if he had just won a prize he really wanted. Andrea ducked her head to look at the menu, not wanting to be affected by that smile.

"I'll just have the grilled chicken spinach salad," she said.

"And for you?" the waitress asked, turning to Donny.

After Donny placed his order, the waitress left them.

Andrea raised her head to see Donny already staring at her.

"What?" she asked self-consciously.

"I was just wondering when I became Mr. Hasgrove," he replied, his voice filled with disappointment.

"It's better that way," she reasoned.

"For who?" he fired back.

She didn't answer.

"I'm sorry, Andrea, it was out of place," Donny apologized.

"It's fine," she replied, giving him a polite smile.

"So, what I wanted to show you, were these. I just need your approval on the final edits, and then I'll be finished by next week." Andrea showed him the photos she had decided on using and ran him through the final design of the website, giving him a demonstration of the ease at which the information would be available to the public.

"Yeah, I mean, it all looks good. I'm not technology smart by any means, but I liked the demonstration of how easy it looks to use. Of course, you have the go-ahead," Donny approved.

She was pleased to know that he liked everything.

After their lunch meeting, Donny walked her toward her house.

"Thanks for stopping by. I'm happy you like the presentation. Everything will be ready by next week," she informed Donny as they stood at her front door.

"Andrea, wait..."

Andrea looked down at the hand that lightly grasped her upper arm, preventing her from opening the door. She turned to look at Donny. As if just realizing that he had touched her, he quickly released her arm as if it were on fire.

"I'm sorry," he apologized.

She shook her head, unable to respond verbally as her heart beat erratically against her chest, and she waited in anticipation for what he had to say to her.

"I know you might not want to hear this now, but I can't...I can't keep it to myself anymore."

The hairs at the nape of her neck and on her forearms stood at attention as goose bumps prickled her skin in anticipation.

"I miss you... I miss our friendship. It was so easy to talk to you, and that's something I've not felt in over ten years," the man before her, raking his hand through his hair, revealed.

Andrea waited with bated breath.

"I really like you, Andrea. I mean a lot. I know you might be hesitant, but somehow I think that you feel this connection that I've felt for you from the very beginning."

"Donny..." she started but couldn't continue. She didn't know what to say.

"Tell me it's a lie, that you don't feel it, and I promise I'll leave you alone," he implored.

Andrea sighed warily. "It's not that simple, Donny, you know that."

"Nothing in life is simple, not if you want it to mean something," he stepped in to say.

Andrea pursed her lips as she cast a doubtful look at him.

"Please, just give me a chance, Drea. Go on a date with me, and we'll take it from there," he pleaded.

She wanted to say yes, to see where this thing could take them, but she couldn't, not right away. She needed to sort out her relationship with her daughter.

"I'll think about it."

Chapter Twenty-One

Andrea was panicking. Why had she allowed her sisters to talk her into accepting the date with Donny? She wasn't ready for a relationship, not right now when the most important one was broken. She needed to be focusing her energy on reconciling her relationship with her daughter.

Her mother and sisters had counseled her to give Rory time to process her feelings. She understood that, but it didn't make it any easier to have her daughter so close and yet so far. Rory was still staying by the inn, and though she ate meals with the family, she barely exchanged more than two words with Andrea.

"Andrea, you're overthinking it," Cora said above her head as she styled her hair. "All you need to focus on is having a good time, not where it will lead."

Andrea sighed sadly. "But how can I enjoy myself knowing that my daughter won't even speak with me?" she bemoaned.

Josephine was crouched down before her, painting her nails, when she looked up at her. "As much as Rory is not speaking to you right now, that girl loves you very much, and she wants you to be happy," she told her with assurance.

"You neglected your own personal happiness to make sure your daughter had everything she needed and was happy without the help of her father. You can't keep neglecting your own happiness, Drea." Cora gave her a meaningful look. "Do you remember the dreams and aspirations book you had back in high school?" she asked.

Andrea nodded, remembering all the dreams she had. One of them was to be married and raise a family.

"This is your chance to tick off some things from that book, Drea. Don't let this be a missed opportunity."

"I love you guys. I don't know what I would do without you here," she expressed. The sisters hugged, feeling their bond being strengthened by their shared experiences.

The sisters resumed what they were doing earlier: Cora putting her hair up into a high bun and Josephine painting her nails. They helped her into the baby blue silk dress they had chosen for her and her strappy heels.

A smile of appreciation graced her lips as she stared at her reflection in the mirror.

"You look absolutely breathtaking, Drea. I'm pretty sure you're going to give Donny a heart attack," Cora spoke, coming up to her.

Andrea laughed at her sister's overgenerous compliment.

"I thought the aim was to get him to take me to dinner, not for me to take him to the hospital."

"In any case, we would still know it had the right effect," Josephine chimed in.

"I love you girls so much," she cheesed.

The doorbell rang fifteen minutes later, and Cora went downstairs to let in Donny while Josephine assisted Andrea down the stairs.

She saw him before he saw her. She felt butterflies stir in

her stomach as she felt warmness travel up her neck before settling in her cheeks. When he saw her, his eyes widened in amazement before shuttering in appreciation.

"You look beautiful. Wow," he expressed, offering her the bouquet of purple and yellow tulips and daffodils.

"Thank you." She blushed, taking the flowers from his hand and bringing them to her face to smell their soft fragrance.

"I'll take these and put them in some water for you," Cora offered, taking the flowers.

"Hi, I'm Josephine. We haven't met yet," her sister greeted Donny with a wide grin.

"Hi, Josephine. It's a pleasure to meet you."

"You didn't tell me he was this handsome." She turned to Andrea with a twinkle in her eyes.

"Thank you, I guess?" Donny said, unsure as the statement had been directed at her sister.

The two left shortly after her sister grilled him and warned him not to make their sister cry, much to her chagrin.

"Did I mention that you look absolutely breathtaking?" Donny asked, briefly looking over at her before turning his attention back to the road.

"I don't mind hearing it a few more times," she encouraged.

"Oh, I plan on it," he returned.

Andrea smiled, feeling blissful.

Donny took her to the restaurant Seaside Hideaway, close to the harbor on Bayshore Drive. She remembered that it had been run by a lovely couple, Dean and Willa Ross. However, upon inquiry, it was revealed that it was now run by their son and his wife.

"So, what made you change your mind to come?" Donny asked her shortly after they were seated.

Andrea took a sip of the ice-cold water before looking at Donny, whose unwavering gaze was already on her.

"My sisters," she confessed. "They can be quite pushy."

At this, he smiled widely. "I'll have to thank them for pushing you then."

Andrea laughed. "You're only going to encourage their continued meddling in our affairs."

"Ah, so it's our affairs now," he spoke, pleased.

Andrea felt her cheeks warm and was sure their color had changed to a rosy pink.

The two talked and laughed as they had their meal. It felt like it had before but even better now that they could freely express their feelings to each other.

The topic of his son did come up, and she agreed to give him time to warm up to her. She told Donny about Rory's father and how telling her the truth was now affecting their relationship.

"Your sisters and your mother are right, Drea. You have to give her the time she needs. At least she's still here. That must count for something," he reasoned.

Andrea shook her head in agreement. "I guess you're right," she responded.

After leaving the restaurant, Donny invited her to walk along the boardwalk with him. She enjoyed the comfortable silence that had fallen between them, and she took the time to admire the beauty of the lights from the shops casting their luminescence on the tranquil surface of the water. She shivered when a soft wind began to blow around them before she felt herself being enveloped in the warmness of Donny's jacket.

She looked up and gave him a grateful smile.

The two settled against the guard rails, listening to the soft push and pull of the waves below.

"I know you said you heard the conversation I had with my son at the cookout, but I think I need to clear some things up," Donny said, breaking the silence.

Andrea looked over at him with caution. "It's okay. You don't have to explain."

"No, I do," he countered, turning to rest his side on the rail so that he was facing her.

Andrea dared not to do the same. She didn't want him to see the anxiety reflected in her eyes.

"I loved my wife, Drea. She was my best friend, literally. We got married right after high school, and for the most part, we had a happy life. The boys adored her, especially Trey. But then she got diagnosed with cancer. She responded positively to treatment for the first year of the disease, but afterward, everything started going downhill. At the time, I was a firefighter. I had to shuffle between being there for her, taking care of our boys, and having a roof over our heads...I would do it again if I had to." Donny sighed.

Andrea turned and placed an encouraging hand on his arm. Donny looked up at her, and her heart broke at the pain she saw there.

Donny gulped down something in his throat and continued. "We didn't tell the boys because we didn't want to burden them with this, but gradually they began to realize that something was wrong. They weren't buying the mommy's just a little under the weather or that her immune system just wasn't as strong as ours, and that's why she had to be spending so much time at the hospital."

Donny paused again to run his hand through his hair. Andrea rubbed his arm in comfort.

"Trey began acting out in school, getting in fights, and I just didn't know what to do anymore." He sighed.

"Peggy decided that they needed to know, and so we finally told them by that time, she was at stage four, and she'd stopped responding to the treatment. Trey wouldn't leave her side because we had in-home treatment. He wasn't going to his classes, and he kept getting into fights, so we had to pull him out to be homeschooled and so that he could spend the time he wanted with her."

Donny paused again and shook his head. He then took in a long breath. Andrea was about to tell him if it was too difficult for him to talk about, he could stop, but then he began speaking again.

"On his tenth birthday, Peggy wanted us to get a birthday cake for him. I forgot to pick it up, and I was at work on a call. She-she...she left home to get it. That's when the accident happened. She was coming back from the bakery when the other driver slammed into her. I got the call, and although the other firefighters tried to prevent me from going to the scene, I had to go. I had to be there for her in that hour."

Donny laughed, but the sound coming from him was mirthless, and Andrea's heart broke a little more for him.

"It's kind of ironic how we knew and were expecting her to die soon, but when she died, it caught us all by surprise and shook us to our core."

Andrea moved her hand over to rub his back.

"I'm so sorry, Donny," she soothed.

Donny gave her a small smile. "After her funeral, he ran away, and when I found him, he looked so broken, and I didn't know what to do, so I promised him that until we got to reunite with her again, it would always only be the three of us— me, him, and Bruce. I promised him that no one would ever take his mother's place."

Donny placed his hand over Andrea's and intertwined their fingers.

"I know it's a lot to take in, and I have some things to sort through with my son, but I also want you to know that I was able to keep the promise for nine almost ten years because I didn't find a reason to revisit it."

Donny took her other hand, causing them to stand completely facing each other. He stared into her eyes as he continued expressing his raw emotions. "No one has had the effect that you have had on me since the first day I met you,

Drea. When I am around you, I forget that there is bad in the world, and when you smile, it makes me feel purpose. Something I haven't felt in a long time."

Andrea couldn't help the smile that came to her lips or her hands from moving under his arms and hugging him to her. She'd never felt the way she felt about Donny, and in this instance, she was unable to express them in words. She just held him close to her heart.

"I really had a great time tonight," Andrea spoke as she looked shyly up at Donny.

"I did too," he confirmed. "Does that mean I can take you out again?"

"I would be worried if you chose not to," she returned.

Donny gave her a charming smile before stepping closer to her. Andrea held her breath, waiting, and when his head descended toward her, she slowly closed her eyes and lifted her face to meet the impending kiss. Only it didn't happen the way she anticipated. Donny's lips met her cheek in a light kiss before he lifted his head and stared into her now opened eyes.

"I'll see you soon," he promised.

Andrea mustered a smile and nodded in return, even though she felt disappointment from not feeling his lips on hers. Still, this was the best date she'd ever had, and she couldn't wait to go out with him again.

After making her way back home, she walked toward the porch. She stopped in her tracks when she realized her daughter was seated on a swing.

Chapter Twenty-Two

"H-hi, sweetie," she greeted as she cautiously walked toward her.

Rory looked up at her mother as she approached. "I need you to set up the zoom appointment with the lawyer," she informed Andrea.

Andrea gave her daughter a small smile of understanding. "Okay, sweetie, I'll do that," she agreed. "Is there anything else that you'd like me to do?"

"No. Just that."

The disappointment that Andrea felt at her daughter's seeming dismissal caused her heart to plummet to the bottom of her chest, but she maintained the smile. "Sounds good, honey. I'll see you in the morning."

"Mom," Rory called out before she'd made more than three steps.

Andrea turned to her daughter with a hopeful expression.

"Can you... can you tell me about him? My father?" she asked.

Andrea's heart broke at the vulnerability in her voice.

"I can," she confirmed, "but I'm afraid you won't like what I have to say," she cautioned.

"Mom, please."

"All right." Andrea sat in the chair opposite her daughter's.

"I met your father at a party I was waitressing at. He was an up-and-coming movie director. They were throwing a party to celebrate the success of his latest film. You could say I caught his eyes... For the next two weeks, he chased me, and I was young and felt special because the attention he was showing me was overwhelming. I felt like I had won the jackpot, and this was another success to rub in my father's face and prove him wrong that I wouldn't make it."

Andrea paused, steeling herself to continue with the darker side of the story.

"When he finally got what he wanted, I woke up to a note that he had to fly out and wouldn't be back for a while. There was also two hundred dollars to take a cab home. After that, every call to him went to voicemail. I missed my period, and subsequently, I took a pregnancy test to find out that I was pregnant... with you. I decided to visit his home, and that's where I found out that not only did he trick me into falling for him, but that he actually had a fiancée that he didn't want to lose. I went through my pregnancy alone and confused."

"I'm sorry, Mom, I didn't know you went through all of that," Rory consoled her.

Andrea gave her a grateful smile.

"When you were four, I brought you to meet him. You were too young for you to remember this. When I got to him, he laughed in my face and said I couldn't prove that he was your father because if I could..."

Andrea felt her heart clench as the words he said to her gave shape vividly to the words and the man who spoke them.

"Anyway, that's in the past," she said, skirting over the thought.

"Mom, please, you're helping me to understand what kind of man he was. Just tell me. I believe I've earned the right to know," Rory implored.

"He alluded that I was loose, even though I was a virgin when I met him. He threatened to have me arrested, and you put into foster care if I ever showed my face to him again. At the time, I was broken, and I didn't want you growing up with the knowledge that your father didn't want you, so I lied. I couldn't bear to see this look that you have on your face now. Not then and still not now."

Andrea reached over and touched her daughter's face, using her thumb to wipe her tears. She gave her a pained look from the guilt of her actions and the hurt it was causing her now.

"I told you he died when you were a baby, and for that, I am sorry. You deserved to know that your father was alive. It was not my place to decide he was dead," she expressed, pained.

Rory sat for a few minutes, running over all the information her mother had just given her as her tears flowed down her face.

Andrea sat with her head down, tears running down her face as she thought about how she messed up. She felt a pair of hands wrap around her in a tight hug.

"I'm sorry that happened to you, Mom," her daughter sobbed against her shoulder. "I wish you didn't have to go through all of what you've been through."

Andrea clung to her daughter as the saltiness of her tears touched her tongue as she pursed her lips in an effort to stop them.

"I don't agree with what you did, but I understand why you

did it, and I don't blame you anymore for doing what you thought was best for me. You were young and going through so much, and still, you made sure I was okay. I watched you sacrifice for my well-being."

The two continued to hug fiercely as their tears continued to flow down their faces.

"I love you, Rory."

"I love you, too, Mom."

* * *

"Where are you taking me?" Andrea asked the man who was leading her by the hand because he had blindfolded her.

"You'll know soon enough," came his reply.

Andrea pouted. She heard Donny laugh as he continued to lead her forward.

After she'd presented the finished website to the fire department, everyone loved it and applauded her efforts of capturing every aspect of their work and for making it enticing to those who would want to make a contribution to the department in any way they could.

Trey, who had been at the department at the time, had complimented her work which had caused hope to spring up in her heart. She caught Donny's look of satisfaction, and she smiled.

Donny had come up to her and gave her a hug to hoots and cheers from the firefighters, and while Trey didn't join in the cheering, he didn't seem angry either, just unsure.

After the presentation, Donny informed her that he had planned a picnic for them, and she readily accepted the invitation.

Now, she was wondering if she'd made the right decision the further away from the noise they went. The serene calmness was welcoming, but without her sense of sight, it was also a frightening experience.

"All right, we're here," Donny gave out, coming behind her to untie the blindfold.

Andrea was awestruck at what was before her. Turning to Donny, she looked at him with incredulity. "How did you find this place?" she asked in wonder.

"When I moved here, I was still grieving, but then I was driving along SW Scenic Heights, and I don't know, I just felt the urge to stop and walk through the forest of trees. The more I walked, the more the clearing came into view, and this is where I ended up," he revealed.

"It's beautiful," she whispered, looking out at the lush meadow with colorful flowers and shrubs permeating the greenness covered by the canopy of trees bordering it. She could also make out a small stream, its gurgling water making its own path from the meadow into the forest.

Donny took her hand, leading her to an area that was flat enough to lay the blanket he had brought.

"When I found this place, I immediately knew that one day everything would be okay again."

Andrea's heart warmed at his words.

"Thank you for sharing this with me," she expressed, patting his arm in gratitude.

Donny took her hand between his and gently squeezed, causing goose bumps to rise.

"You're special, and you are worth sharing a lot of things with," he spoke sincerely.

Andrea couldn't stop the smile that graced her lips as her heart soared with his words.

"I want to share something else with you," he informed her gently.

"You mean apart from the food?" she asked jokingly.

Donny chuckled. "We'll get to that soon. This is more food for your heart," he told her.

Andrea sat up straighter, intrigued by what he said.

"I wrote something for you," he said, going into his pocket and removing a folded sheet of paper.

"I'm no Shakespeare, but I hope I have expressed it vividly enough for you to understand how I feel about you."

Andrea perked up. She folded her legs and sat on the back of her knees before she leaned forward, putting most of her weight on her palms.

"Here it goes," he announced, the quiver in his voice giving away his nervousness.

"One day, my sun went away
The moon refused to rise
The stars imploded
One day my world stopped turning, and I didn't know if
I would ever feel the wind on my face again or
The waters between my toes
The grains of sand grazing my fingertips
Then you crashed into me like a whirlwind on a normally windless day
And you brought with you the sun, the moon, and the stars
How could I ever try to resist?
When you brought with you everything I was missing
But never knew I could ever get back
Now that you're with me like this
I can't imagine a life and you not in it
A song and you aren't the muse
A carefree thought, and it doesn't echo your name
I love you in this season, and I know I will love you out of season
I will love you until the end of time."

Andrea could not contain the tears that flowed down her

face as her heart bubbled with the joy she felt at finding someone that valued her so much.

"If I knew this was the reaction I would have gotten, I would have thought twice about sharing it," Donny murmured, unsure. "Drea, please don't cr—"

Andrea cupped his face and kissed him deeply, willing him to feel how moved she was by his poem and how much she felt for him.

"I guess that means I'll be writing a whole lot more then."

The two had burst into laughter at the comment before she peppered his face with her kisses once more.

For the remainder of the picnic, the two talked, joked, and cuddled.

When Donny dropped her off at home, Andrea couldn't help the smile she'd been sporting since the picnic.

"Someone's happy, happy," Cora observed.

"I am," she confirmed.

Cora grinned as she pulled her sister toward the kitchen. "You have to tell me everything that happened on your little love picnic."

"What's happening?" Josephine, who was already seated around the island, asked.

"Drea is going to tell us about her magical time with Donny," Cora replied.

"Okay, this calls for Ben and Jerry's ice cream," Josephine said excitedly, removing the tub of ice cream from the freezer.

Cora went to the drawer and removed three spoons. She handed one to each sister, and they sat scooping the frozen treat into their mouths.

The sisters sat listening to Andrea recount the time she had with Donny and how much she felt as if this was the start of something lasting.

"Oh, I can't wait for another little niece or nephew that I can get to spoil," Cora gushed.

167

Andrea reared back in horror. "Whoa, Cora, slow down a little. Who said anything about babies?"

The three of them carried on laughing and sharing stories. Andrea had never imagined this happening. It was funny how things always worked out. She was just grateful to be home with her family.

Epilogue

Andrea, Cora, Josephine, and Rory sat at the table going over some great sites where Rory could take her bridal photos if she chose to have the event in Oak Harbor.

"What are you girls doing?" their mother asked as she stepped through the door.

"Hey, Mom. We were just going through some photos. You know, to show Rory the best the island has to offer," Cora explained.

"That's great. Did you show her Dugualla?" she asked, coming to take a seat.

"Yeah, that's a great one. Jo, pull that one up," Andrea instructed.

Josephine typed in the name, pulling up the state park that offered a wonderful view of the bay and mountain range in the background.

"How are you feeling, Mom?" Andrea asked, recalling that last week she had two episodes of muscle spasms that had made her feel down.

"I'm okay. I guess we can write this off as a good week," she replied with a grin.

Andrea reached over and grasped her mother's hand in encouragement while Cora sat beside her hugging her to her side.

"We're glad, Mom. We know it won't always be easy, but we'll always be here for you."

Becky gave her daughters a grateful smile.

"You may not agree with me, but you girls are my heroes. To think that you all left home with nothing but what you brought with you, and still you persevered to be where you are now. I'm not sure I would have been able to do it. I've ever only known one life and one way, and that was being married to your father and living here."

Andrea rounded the island to embrace her mother.

"Mom." She sighed as the others joined in the hug.

"Oh, I had the call with the lawyer last night," Rory informed the group of women.

"How did it go, sweetie?" Andrea asked, forgetting that the appointment had been yesterday.

"If being half a million dollars richer means that it went well, then it went well," she revealed with a wide grin.

The woman stared at her wide-eyed.

"Oh my God, that's...that's great," Andrea managed to get out. She was happy for her daughter and, in some way, thankful to David for finally doing the right thing in his death.

The other women congratulated her before they settled back in their seats.

"I have more good news," she said, causing the chatter to stop again and for all eyes to be turned to her.

"I have decided to have the wedding here. I spoke with James already, and he is in total agreement."

Just like that, the merriment went up tenfold.

Andrea placed her hand over her chest as she stared

lovingly at her daughter, but she couldn't force any words through her lips.

"Mom, aren't you happy?" Rory asked, concerned.

"I am, sweetie, but only if you are sure."

Rory held her mother's hand and squeezed.

"I'm very sure," she confirmed.

With that, Andrea brought her daughter to her chest and hugged her with all her love. Afterward, Rory left to meet up with Kerry's daughter.

Once all the commotion settled down, the sisters left the house to go visit the flower garden.

"I think we should do something for Mom's birthday, maybe keep the tradition Dad started," Andrea suggested to her sisters.

"That's a great idea," Cora responded, and Josephine nodded in agreement.

"I thought we could all choose to plant a different species of rose. If we do it now, I think they would bloom in time to surprise her," she continued to say.

The sisters agreed before sitting on the raised platform.

"Guys, I have something to share with you, but I don't know where to begin."

Andrea and Cora looked at their sister in concern.

"It is about the accident..." Josephine paused.

She breathed in deeply before continuing.

"I suspected Nicholas wasn't himself during the accident," she said slowly.

"What do you mean?" Cora asked as Andrea looked at her sister, perplexed.

"I'm saying that... oh, it doesn't matter now." Josephine averted her eyes, but her sisters could see that what she was about to say was something possibly earth-shattering.

"Jo, I'm sure it's not nothing if you brought it up," Cora spoke softly.

Josephine looked back at her sisters with tears in her eyes. "I just feel so ashamed," she sobbed.

They rushed to her side, hugging her closely.

"You don't have to talk about it now, Jo. Just know that we're here when you're ready," Cora soothed her.

Josephine gave her a grateful smile, squeezing the hand on her cheek.

They decided to change the subject to talk about their plans for their mother's birthday some more instead of focusing on more heartache.

"Let's go for a ride on Dad's old boat," Josephine suggested.

"You mean the *Silver Bullet*," Cora replied.

"He renamed the boat?"

"Yeah, Jo, he did," Andrea confirmed.

Josephine put her hand to her mouth as a wave of sadness and happiness washed over her at the same time.

The sisters gave her a knowing look as they had all felt the same way.

After donning swimsuits under their clothes, they made their way down to the dock and boarded the boat.

Josephine ran her hand lovingly over the words painted on the boat, and Cora and Drea looked on in understanding.

"Great going, Dad," she threw into the wind.

Andrea, who stood at the wheel, took the boat out. She brought it back to the south side of the Camano Islands so that they could enjoy the alcove in privacy. The sisters enjoyed the magnificent view of the mountain ranges in the background of the blue-green waters as the boat seamlessly sliced through the waves.

Andrea brought the boat to a stop and began mooring it about one mile away from the alcove.

"God, I've missed this," Josephine expressed as she sat with her legs dangling from the side of the boat as she looked out across the expanse of the ocean.

"I can't believe we stayed away as long as we did, and yet, while everything moved forward, it's like it was just waiting for us to come back to pick up where we left off," Cora mused.

The others nodded in agreement.

They all stripped down to their swimsuits before diving into the calm blue waters.

Andrea felt carefree as she enjoyed the warmth of the water.

"Race me," she heard Josephine challenge Cora, who had been floating on her back.

"I'll be the official," Andrea offered.

"All right," Cora agreed, flipping over. "I must warn you, though, Jo, I've still got it from high school."

"And I don't?" Josephine rebuffed.

"All right, contestants, take your places," Andrea ordered in an official tone.

The sisters snorted at her act.

"On your mark... set... go!"

The two sisters took off toward the boat, and Andrea stayed back, watching them go with a smile on her lips.

Josephine was the first to touch the boat, making her the winner.

"Better luck next time, Grandma," she teased her sister.

"Why, you little..."

Cora took off after her sister, who swam away, evading her.

Andrea laughed at their antics. As her laughter died down, a smile of satisfaction settled on her face as she realized that her family was together again. She was in the phase of young love, and she couldn't be happier.

If she chose optimism to think that the glass was half full rather than half empty, then as she looked at her sisters laughing and splashing each other before her, then everything was falling into place, and she couldn't be happier.

Coming Next in the Oak Harbor Series

You can pre order Summertime Forgiveness

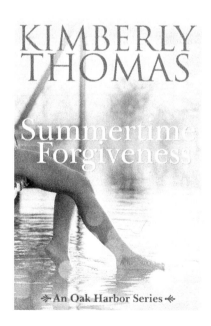

Other Books by Kimberly

The Archer Inn Series

Connect with Kimberly Thomas

Facebook
Newsletter
BookBub
Amazon

To receive exclusive updates from Kimberly, please sign up to be on her Newsletter!

CLICK HERE TO SUBSCRIBE

Printed in Great Britain
by Amazon

84609616R00108